SHARK 2

CATHERINE BANKS

Thank you to my amazing husband who continues to support me. I love you and your amazing cuddles.

PREFACE

This was first published on Vella, so you may notice that these chapters are shorter than my normal ones. That is due to the episodic format. Don't worry, this is the complete second book, but be warned you may zoom through it with chapters being shorter.

Happy reading! :)

I

"The jellyfish are out performing me," I whined as Theo and I ate our tacos.

Theo, my best friend and a powerful mage, set her margarita down. "What? I thought the kids loved you?"

"The kids do love me, but the parents love the jellyfish more and started coming on dates there! How am I supposed to compete with that?" As a shark shifter who couldn't shift her teeth well, jobs were limited. So, I'd taken a job at an aquarium as their tiger shark. Most sharks didn't do well in captivity, so this was the only aquarium to have a tiger shark on exhibit. I spent my days in shark form, swimming around the aquarium, then my nights with my boyfriends at our house.

It was still surreal to be able to say that. A year ago, I was sleeping in the aquarium in shark form at night because I didn't have a place to live, and I was wondering if I was going to be single the rest of my life.

"Is there something you are famous for … tiger sharks, not you specifically?" she asked.

I closed my mouth since I'd been about to say something dirty regarding myself, which made her laugh.

"There you two are," Grant said as he walked inside the Mexican restaurant we frequented on Tuesdays, and sat beside me. Grant was a dragon shifter, a mostly average looking man with talented fingers, and one of my boyfriends.

I leaned over and he met me halfway to kiss my lips. "Where've you been?"

"The octopus sprayed ink out of the tank again," he grumbled and crunched on a chip.

"Where's Reed?" I asked and looked at the door, but he hadn't walked in. Reed was a werewolf, insanely hot with a sixpack of abs I enjoyed stroking, striking eyes, and was another of my boyfriends.

Grant and Reed had taken jobs as janitors at the aquarium I worked at to not only make some money, but also to stay close to me.

My other two boyfriends, twin brothers Jong-min and Jong-hyun, took a job at my adoptive parents' restaurant, helping them cook Asian cuisine and serving customers. They'd looked for jobs for a bit and then Mother had ordered them to help since she and Father were older. That was all it had taken to crush the twins' desire to say no. Family was extremely important to them and taking care of their elders was ingrained in their brains.

"He's—" Grant didn't get to finish as Reed walked in, sauntering across the restaurant and gaining every female eye as he did.

"Can you make them stop strutting so much? It's so distracting," Theo hissed and chugged her margarita.

I snickered and made a kissy face so Reed would kiss me before he sat down.

"I heard Trinity is giving you trouble again," I said.

Reed growled and nodded. "She's a jealous bitch!"

Trinity was the oldest octopus in our aquarium, and when the guys didn't give her treats, or saw them give treats to other creatures, she made messes for them to clean up.

If I didn't know better, I'd have assumed she was a shifter, but Trinity was a normal octopus, they were just really intelligent creatures.

"Stop feeding other creatures in front of her," I said with a scoff. "She's not the only one who gets jealous when she sees you feeding the asshole jellyfish."

Theo spit out her drink and coughed violently as the alcohol burned her throat.

Reed patted her back while Grant and I cleaned up the sprayed liquid.

"Oh, my god! Could you not say such ridiculous things while I'm in the middle of drinking?" Theo gasped, and tapped her wig to make sure it was still in its correct place.

"It's not ridiculous!" I snapped. "Have you ever watched your boyfriends fawn over your enemies? It's cruel and unusual punishment!"

"Enemies?" Grant asked. "What are you talking about?"

"Hey, guys," Charles greeted Grant and Reed. Charles was our usual server when we came here and knew better than to bother bringing menus, since we got the same things every single time. "The girls already put in your food order, but you want your usual drinks, too?"

Grant and Reed nodded.

"More salsa, please," Theo ordered.

"And guac and chips!" I added quickly. With a dragon and werewolf here, we were going to run out of guacamole and chips soon.

Charles smiled, nodded, and went off to put in our orders.

"So, are you trying to say that if you were an octopus, you would spray ink out of your area to force us to clean it up, too, because you're jealous of the jellyfish?" Grant asked, drawing my attention back to him.

I shrugged a shoulder innocently. "Maybe."

He chuckled and shook his head. "My beautiful disaster, we only feed them treats because it makes them go into a frenzy, which makes the visitors happy."

My eyes narrowed and I bared my serrated teeth at him. "Exactly! You're helping those tentacled freaks get more attention than they deserve!"

Reed burst into laughter, clutching his stomach as he laughed loudly, and almost fell out of his chair.

My lips pursed in a pout. "Sure, laugh it up. My pain is super funny."

"Jong-min and Jong-hyun are going to meet us at Silver's after dinner. They had some important discussion with your parents that couldn't be delayed, apparently," Grant said, ignoring my craziness.

My eyes widened. "What?" That was news to me. Mother and Father hadn't said anything to me.

Reed's phone rang and he dismissed himself, promising to meet back up with us.

The serious expression on his face worried me, but I left it alone.

Once we finished eating, we headed to Silver's bar. Silver, an old ogre who was a pseudo father to me, ran a bar where I often hustled unsuspecting tourists out of money. Reed had still been on the phone, and said he'd meet us there.

Tonka, the half-troll bouncer, nodded at us as we approached. "The twins are inside already."

The line of people waiting to get in grumbled as we bypassed the line, but Theo, Grant, and I ignored them.

"Thanks, Tonka." I patted his massive arm as I walked by.

"Good crowd for being a shark tonight," he whispered.

"Thanks for the tip," I replied.

Theo patted his upper chest. "Just the tip."

Tonka groaned and shook his head. "Get away from me, dirty minded witch."

She and I threw our heads back and laughed while Grant chuckled.

The bar was full of all kinds of beings: orcs, goblins, mages, and multiple types of aquatic and land shifters. I even spotted what looked like a few humans. About half of the clientele were regulars, like us, but the other half were college-aged tourists, many of which were already several drinks in judging by their stumbling.

At the main bar stood two of the most perfect specimens, feline shifters with rare magic, dark hair, hooded eyes, and both in tank tops and shorts.

"You're drooling," Theo teased.

"Do you blame me?" I asked.

Jong-hyun and Jong-min spotted us. Jong-hyun smiled while Jong-min scowled.

I skipped over and kissed them each. "Hello."

"You're late," Jong-min chastised.

"We didn't set a specific time," I countered.

"Kass," Silver greeted. "You want the usual or my new drink?"

"New!" Theo shouted before I could answer.

Silver laughed, grabbed some bottles from the bar behind him, and started mixing something while hiding the bottles so we couldn't see what he put in it.

"Was your food good?" Jong-hyun asked. His arm slid around my lower back and I stepped into him.

"Yes," I answered, nodding. "It was definitely needed after the day I had."

"The parents keep diverting the kids away from you to see the jellyfish still?" he guessed.

I fake sniffled. "Yeah, and Grant was giving them snacks!"

He fake gasped. "No!"

Grant rolled his eyes as he squeezed between us at the bar. "I'm sorry, but it is part of my job."

"What if they end up not needing me anymore and then I'll be out of a job?" I was mostly kidding, but there was a small part of me worried about that possibility.

"Well, you better make some money as your other shark form then," Jong-min said from behind me.

I spun, a small smile on my face to keep my sharp, serrated, shark teeth mostly hidden. No matter how hard I tried to shift them, they never became dull, like a human's, while I could get the rest of my body to do so. Often, if my teeth were exposed, people avoided me. Somehow, my four amazing boyfriends were able to overlook it. "Being a pool shark is my favorite form."

"Because it earns you the most money," Reed, my drop-dead gorgeous werewolf shifter boyfriend said as he joined us. He threw his arms around me and pulled me into a bone-crunching hug.

"You guys are going to make me sick," Theo muttered.

"Did you miss me?" Reed asked.

I nodded. "Grant was super mean to me today."

"Here we go," Grant sighed.

Reed kissed my cheek and asked, "Want me to kick his ass?"

Watching them fight was incredibly fun.

"Help me hustle some guys?" I countered.

"You got it."

"Girls, your drinks," Silver said, and set two swirling green drinks on the bar top.

Quickly, I extricated myself from Reed and gently pushed Jong-min to the side so Theo could stand at the bar with me.

We both stared into the drinks, eyes wide.

"Looks like poison," I whispered out of the side of my mouth.

Theo nodded. "It swirls and sparkles. I didn't know a non-magical liquid could do both."

"Flip a coin to see who tries it first?"

She scoffed. "I know you've got a weighted coin."

We both heard Silver sigh, but we ignored him, focused on our silliness and fun.

"Drink it together and if it is poison, we'll die together?" I suggested.

She nodded and we simultaneously picked up the drinks, clinked the rims against each other, and then downed them in one gulp.

Fruity ecstasy exploded on my tongue, down my throat, and into my stomach. A vision of a perfectly warm, sunny beach with just a slight breeze flashed before my eyes before it was replaced with a sense of euphoria.

Theo and I exhaled softly in chorus, leaned our shoulders against each other, and our smiles grew.

"What the fuck did you put in that?" Jong-min demanded.

"Pixie dust," Theo replied and leaned on the bar with a lazy smile. "Silver, old boy, you've been holding out on us."

"It's Pixie Lite," Silver said. "A version that isn't addictive and doesn't have the negative side effects, aside from adding 100 calories to each drink."

"Theo," a rumbling voice greeted.

We all turned to face the newcomer and my smile wilted, though the Pixie Lite was doing its job of keeping me relaxed and not able to snarl like I wanted.

Tristan, a dolphin shifter with tan skin, light wavy hair, and teal eyes, smiled at Theo.

"Tristan," she straightened, "what are you doing here?"

"Why are you talking to him like you are friends?" I asked.

Theo flinched. "I was going to tell you—"

Leaning closer to her, I asked, "Are you dating a fish corpse fucker?"

"He doesn't do that," she snapped. Her mouth dropped and she cringed. "Kass, I—"

"Kass, I found an open table to teach you how to play pool," Reed said loud enough half of the bar heard him. "Now that you're good and drunk, it's the perfect time for you to learn."

A table of guys just at the edge of my vision watched and whispered to each other as Reed put an arm around my waist and lead me into the room with the pool tables, forcing me away from Theo and the corpse fucker.

Theo, my best friend, was dating a dolphin shifter. My best friend was dating one of my enemies.

"He isn't an enemy. You don't even know him," Reed whispered in my ear as he walked around me to grab a cue.

Had I said that out loud?

"He's a dolphin," I said, and folded my arms across my chest.

"You're being racist," he chided as he racked the balls. "It's not a good look."

Bending over, I lined up my shot and asked, "How do I look now?"

Heat filled his gaze as he looked at me. "You'd look even better tied up on my bed."

My shot went wild at his statement and I barely broke the rack.

Reed chuckled smugly, walked around me, and bent over to take his shot. "Does that suggestion entice you, Kass?"

He hit four balls in a row into the pockets before finally missing.

I saw the guys who'd been watching us walk in and bent over the table with my arm up at a weird angle. "I shoot like this?"

Reed's smile widened, but when he looked up at the guys behind me, the smile completely disappeared. "Preston? What are you doing here? How did you find me?"

The guy in the doorway crossed his arms, a deep frown on his face.

"It's time to come home, Reed. Time to claim your mate."

2

The stranger Reed had called Preston was massive, almost as big as Tonka, had black hair braided close against his head, and a matching beard, also braided. On either side of him were muscular males with ice cold eyes and deep scowls. They didn't look like they wanted to sit down for a nice chat and a drink. The Pixie Lite had hit me harder than I'd realized to have ever considered them for a target to hustle.

"Mate?" I demanded, standing upright, and feeling fully sober.

Reed set the cue down and stepped between the strangers and me. "I'm not going back. I made that clear when I left. I have no interest in an assigned mate."

Back? Were these fellow werewolves from his clan? What did he mean "assigned mate?"

The trio walked closer to us.

"You don't get to decide that," Preston snarled.

"I've got a pack and a bond already," Reed said sternly. "Plus, I was exiled, remember?"

"Your exile is now lifted," Preston said.

"Wh-what?"

The shock in Reed's tone was evident.

He looked down at his feet and back at me, conflicting emotions in his eyes.

Was he going to leave me?

Preston grabbed Reed's arm and pulled him away from me.

I partially shifted, my head turning fully shark, but kept my human arms as I punched Preston in the nose while grabbing Reed with my other hand.

"Tonka!" Zara, one of Silver's adopted daughters who I considered a sister, yelled when she saw me as she stepped inside through the side door.

Immediately, Tonka, Theo, and my other boyfriends ran into the room.

One of the other men tried to punch me, but Reed had finally snapped out of his shock and kicked him away.

"Don't touch her!" he roared.

Tonka grabbed Preston and shoved him towards the side door. "You three, out!"

"We'll be seeing you soon, Reed," Preston called over his shoulder.

The door shut and you could have heard a pin drop.

Reed turned to me and ran his hands down my arms. "Are you hurt?"

No matter how hard I tried, I couldn't shift back to my human form. The anxiety and fear that Reed might leave was too much. "I need to go," I said and ran out of the front entrance, ignoring the voices calling my name and the shouting people as I barreled by them.

I continued to run across town, through the park, ignoring Captain Two Teeth and his shark pirate crew, across the beach, and into the water. As soon as the gloriously warm water closed over my head, my body fully shifted and I let myself drift lazily along the pier.

Running was childish, I knew that, but the look Reed had given me was seared into my brain.

Reed hadn't mentioned his exile to me, but there was a lot we didn't know about each other still. Well, he knew way more about me than I knew about him, thanks to Bastian showing up.

Once I'd calmed down enough to shift back, I would sit down with Reed and talk to him.

Not being able to shift back wasn't a common occurrence for me and I hoped part of it had been due to the Pixie Lite.

A huge shadow covered me, snapping me out of my numbness as my survival instincts kicked in. Something that cast a huge shadow over me like that could eat me and that was not something I wanted to happen. Swimming under the pier for safety, I looked around, but quickly realized it had to have been something flying since I was near the top of the water and nothing that large could swim above me.

Peering out from beneath the pier, I saw Grant circling overhead.

I swam out from beneath the pier, beached myself, and shifted into my human form. Not bothering to get up, I waited for him to land.

He spotted me quickly, shifted into his human form

thirty feet up, and did a superhero landing on the beach ten feet away from me. "Are you okay?"

I sighed and put my arm over my face. "I think the Pixie Lite and stress of the situation prevented me from shifting back. I ran here to see if it would help."

"Are you hurt?" he asked and sat beside me, keeping only his feet in the water.

"No."

"What did they say to upset you guys? Reed wouldn't talk to us."

"Did ... did he leave?" I asked, my throat constricted as I asked and it became hard to swallow.

"Leave? He left the bar to try to find you, we all did. Kass, what's going on?"

"They rescinded his exile and told him he has to return to claim his mate," I answered, dropped my arm, and looked at him with tears in my eyes. "Is he going to go?"

Grant's eyes widened and he stood. "Shit." He turned towards the city and pulled his cell phone out, calling someone. Whoever answered, he didn't bother with formalities, just said, "I found her. Meet at the house. Tell the others."

His response was not instilling confidence in me about the possibility of Reed leaving.

"Grant, if he leaves ... will you three go, too?" I got to my feet and brushed the sand off, once again glad I could shift my scales to look like clothes when necessary. Grant and the others could magic clothes on themselves. I was trying to do it, but was only successful on rare occasions.

Grant put his phone away, turned around, and hugged

me. "I'm not going to abandon you, Kass. Never. Come on, let's go home and talk to Reed."

3

Grant and I were the first ones home, which gave me time to shower and dress.

It also gave me time to stress even more, which I did not like.

I sat on the couch in the living room, my legs folded up beneath me and one of Grant's big hoodie sweatshirts on for some comfort.

Jong-hyun and Jong-min came in together, heads leaned close as they whispered. They sat on the couch opposite me, deep frowns on their faces.

"Where's Reed?" Grant asked as he sat beside me. He made sure our legs touched, giving me comfort through touch, and giving himself comfort as well. Shifters were big on physical affection for comfort.

"Here," Reed answered as he came in through the back door behind me.

Reed and Grant were the first I had developed a connection with. They were the ones who had made me feel most welcomed in this quartet. Losing one of them would severely damage our connection.

"What happened tonight?" Jong-min asked and sat up straight.

Reed sat in the reclining chair to my right and ran a hand through his hair, disheveling it even more. "My pack came for me."

"We're your pack," Grant snapped.

"Easy," Jong-min whispered.

"I'm sorry I ran off," I said quickly. "The drink hit me harder than I realized and I wasn't able to shift back and it freaked me out."

Reed wouldn't look at me, his eyes focused on the coffee table before us. "They've lifted my exile."

"Good for them," Grant said. "You warned them that when you left, you would never return."

Reed raised his head and narrowed his eyes. "So, you're telling me that if your flight came for you, you wouldn't consider leaving?"

"No, I wouldn't," Grant said. He growled deep in his chest and stood. "The three of you are my clan now. Those bastards may share bloodlines with me, but they don't care about me. They only care about what I can or cannot provide them."

So, Reed *was* considering leaving.

"Is it because I'm not a werewolf?" I asked.

"Our birthrate has decreased every decade," Reed whispered. "Soon, there may be no werewolves."

Ouch.

"That's not your fault," Jong-hyun said. "You providing a litter won't change that."

"My litter could help us repopulate," Reed argued.

His litter ...

"I thought you loved me," I whispered, tears burning my eyes.

Reed shoved a hand through his hair and closed his eyes. "I do love you, Kass, but—"

"I'm going to bed," I announced and stood. I stumbled a bit and they all reached out towards me. "No!" I snapped and spun away from all of them. "I need to sleep. Sorry. Guess the Pixie Lite doesn't work well for me. Sorry."

I ran up to my room, shutting and locking the door just in time as the tears flooded. We weren't officially mates yet, but we were courting. I had expected to finalize our bond soon, but now ... now I didn't know what was going to happen.

"Kass," Reed called through the door and sighed. "Please, don't cry. I haven't decided yet. This is all crazy and out of the blue and I don't know what to do." He pushed against my door and then slid down it, likely sitting against the door. "At least try to see it from my point of view. What if the Atlanteans suddenly came to you and told you that your exile was lifted and you could return? Wouldn't you consider going back? What if you returning could prevent your extinction?"

"I'm almost extinct as it is," I whispered. "And I'll never be welcomed back to a place that I can weaken so much." Taking a deep breath I added, "You have to do what's right for you and if I'm not what's right ... I just have to accept that."

"Baby, it's not you. There's nothing wrong with you or anything, you—"

I interrupted him, not wanting him to continue. "I need to sleep before work. Please leave."

"Kass, don't shut me out, please."

"I can't change what I am. I'm a shark, I'm not even a land shifter. If you care about repopulating, why aren't you dating a human?"

He didn't respond.

"When you've made your decision, you know where to find me."

"Kass," he pounded on the door.

Talking more tonight wouldn't accomplish anything, so I jumped into the water tank in my room and shifted into my shark form, letting my mind blank as I swam in circles.

Reed was gone before I left the house, but the others wouldn't say where he'd gone. They all wore somber expressions as we went to work.

Try as I might, I couldn't get excited by the kids coming to see me or the other visitors smiling at me.

Halfway through the day, I saw Reed's former pack enter, eyes scanning everything.

There were still three hours left before I was supposed to be off work, but I didn't want to miss saying bye if he was leaving with them.

No, he wouldn't leave without saying goodbye. I had to trust that he would do the right thing, in that at least.

Turning off my human brain, I resumed swimming in lazy circles around the aquarium. It was a relatively quiet day, with no schools visiting, so the day went by in a blur.

When it was time to shift and climb out of the tank, my anxiety returned, and I had to keep counting my breaths to avoid a panic attack.

Warm arms wrapped around me from behind, hugging me back against an even warmer chest. "It's going to be alright," Grant whispered in my ear.

"I'm hungry," I said, instead of responding about Reed. "What should we have for dinner tonight?"

"Sushi?" he suggested.

I spun, mouth open and eyes wide. "You mean it?" We rarely had sushi because it was expensive, but it was one of my favorite things to eat. And yes, it was different than eating fish right out of the sea.

He nodded and smiled. "Yep. My treat. It's been a long time since I've had a date with you, just the two of us."

That was true. I hadn't gone on individual dates with them in a while. That was something I would need to rectify.

I looped my arm through his and had to restrain myself from skipping. "Which sushi place are we going to?" There were two that we liked, but one was my absolute favorite.

"Your favorite, of course," he said. "Only the best for my girl."

Resting my head against his shoulder, I looked up at his side profile. We were still courting, but I had made up my mind that I wanted him, them, as my mates. If I could, I'd seal the bond right now with him.

"I love you," I whispered.

He paused, hand raised to push open the door to exit the aquarium, looked down at me, and said, "I love you, too, Kass." He pushed open the door and we paused when we found Reed's pack members gathered around Reed.

Reed looked up, our eyes connected, and I tugged Grant away, averting my gaze. "Come on, let's go on our date."

4

"We just received our invitations!" Grant yelled as he ran into the living room.

Jong-min and Jong-hyun cuddled on each side of me on the couch, binge watching a drama show they'd introduced me to.

"We got in again?" Jong-min asked, sitting up and nearly making me fall off the couch due to his quick movement.

"Invitation to what?" I asked.

"Only the biggest poker tournament in the state!" Jong-hyun yelled. "I can't believe we all got in. I was sure Grant wouldn't get an invite."

Grant scowled. "I'm a great poker player."

Jong-min and Jong-hyun chuckled simultaneously.

"I didn't know you guys played poker in tournaments." I sat up. "How long have you been doing that?"

"Since we turned eighteen," Grant answered. "Jong-hyun made it to the finals two years ago."

I turned to Jong-hyun, mouth open. "You're a card shark? I'm so upset that you've hidden this from me for so long. We're both sharks!"

He smiled and kissed my cheek. "Yes, we're both sharks in one way."

"When is the tournament?" Jong-min asked Grant.

"Next week. Apparently, since we had two forwarding addresses, it took longer than usual to receive our invitations," Grant answered.

"Why aren't they electronic at this point?" I wondered aloud.

"That is a good question and something I'll bring up to them when we attend," Jong-min said.

I smiled wide. "Did you just agree that I had a good question? Is it my birthday or something?"

He muttered something in another language that sounded vaguely like the word for brat.

"Where is the tournament?" I asked instead of pestering Jong-min more.

"Up north, about a five hour drive from here," Jong-hyun answered as he looked over Grant's shoulder at the invitation. "We'll fly, since that flight is only an hour."

Realization hit me.

"How long will you guys be gone?" Some tournaments happened in one day, while others could be spaced out over two days or even up to a week. I hadn't been apart from them since the Bastian incident.

Would time away from me remind them of their past lives, the times before they'd met me, when they were a solid unit? Would it remind them what it was like and cause them to leave me? Would this be the nail in the coffin of our relationship? Would this be when Reed left?

Jong-min turned to me, his brows furrowed, and asked, "You don't want to come with us?"

My mouth opened and closed a couple of times, like a fish out of water. "I can go with you?"

"If you're worried about work, I can talk to—" Grant started, but I interrupted him.

"No, I'm not worried about work. I just ... didn't think you'd want me to go, I guess." Admitting it made me immediately embarrassed, but it was good for me to be vulnerable with them sometimes.

"It'll be inland, no ocean nearby," Jong-hyun commented. "Can you handle that for a few days?"

A few days away from the sea ...

"I actually haven't been away from the ocean before," I admitted. Could I handle not having salt water?

Jong-min had his phone out, searching for something on the internet, but since he was so far away, I couldn't read it.

"I would be willing to try," I said. "I should be able to handle being away from the ocean, since I don't *need* it to survive. I've just never had the opportunity to travel away from it before."

"It's not just traveling away from it, Kass. We're going to a desert," Grant said softly.

A desert?

"We can discuss that later, what's important is that you *want* to go with us and we want you to go, too," Jong-hyun said.

"It would be a week," Jong-min said, finally answering my original question.

A week away from the ocean, at the desert.

"I-Is Reed going to go with you?" I asked softly, looking down at my hands in my lap.

"Go with them where?" Reed asked and walked into the room. He wore a black tank top and a pair of grey sweatpants. My eyes immediately dropped to the sweatpants, but I jerked them back up to his eyes. His lips twitched on one side, a knowing smirk almost forming, before he resumed frowning.

"Here," Grant said and held out an envelope to Reed.

Reed read it, his eyes widening slightly. "This is perfect," he whispered.

"Perfect?" Grant asked.

Reed glanced at me before turning his entire body to focus on Grant. "Yes, I was looking for a way to stall the pack without outright turning them down and this is a perfect way to do that."

So, he was still considering it. That ... hurt.

Maybe it wasn't a good idea for me to go with them.

I stood and smoothed down my pants. "I'll leave you four to discuss your trip. I'm going to go for a swim. All this talk about deserts has me sweating."

It wasn't a complete lie. I had started sweating when talking about being away from the ocean and inside a desert for a week.

"Have a good swim," Reed said without even looking at me.

Grant's hands balled into fists at his side, eyes narrowing at Reed.

Jong-hyun's hands started to glow pink and his nails turned into claws.

"Thanks," I replied in a chipper tone, trying to defuse the others, at least until I left.

Running out of the house might have been childish, but even this predator knew when to flee.

I jogged all the way to the pier, but instead of diving into the water, I sat on the end of the pier and dangled my feet over the edge, kicking them back and forth. Folding my arms atop the wooden plank in front of me, I rested my head on my arm, and let out a long sigh.

Leather boots stopped beside me. "I haven't heard that type of sigh from you in a long while," Silver said. Slowly, the old ogre sat down beside me, dangling his legs like mine.

"You remember when we used to come talk here?" I asked him, staring out at the surfers enjoying the waves.

"Aye," he replied. "You thought you'd live the rest of your life alone and never find love."

I laughed humorlessly. "Looks like that might still come true."

"Because of those wolves?" he asked.

Flipping my head to my other arm, I looked at him with raised brows.

He smiled, the piercing on his broken tusk rattling as he smiled wide. "I'm a bartender, which means I hear a lot and see a lot. More than most people realize."

That information was getting filed away for further discussion later.

"I don't know that much about their pasts, even still, but apparently he was banished and now they're rescinding it so he can come back, claim a mate, and have a litter of pups," I explained.

"The werewolf population has been on a decline the last decade," Silver said and rubbed his jaw while he looked out over the ocean.

So, it was true.

"It's hard when your blood comes calling, shouting out for help, even when you've already written them off," Silver said. He tapped his broken tusk. "I've dealt with it a time or two myself, so I can understand his conflicting feelings."

"How do you know he has conflicting feelings?"

He scoffed and looked down at me. "Anyone can see that boy cares about you, Kass. He's been head over heels, following you like a starved puppy given a treat, since he saw you. It weren't no surprise that you started courting. I mean, he went into the fracking ocean to try to save you."

"We have a connection, one I don't really understand, but maybe it's better if I let him go. I don't want to stop him from being able to return to his pack."

Silver draped an arm around my shoulders and squeezed me once. "Child, you're not stopping him from anything. The fact he hasn't left yet is proof he cares about you. You cannot make the decision for him, so the best thing to do is treat him like nothing has changed. Continue going on your dates and making goo-goo eyes at each other. It's up to him to decide what to do."

"Well, now they've been invited to a poker tournament in the desert and they invited me to go. A week in the desert, away from the ocean. I've ... I've never been away from it before."

Silver frowned, dropped his arm, and looked down at the water before us. "I can't say for certain how you'll feel, as I'm not a shifter, but I think you'd be able to handle it. It likely won't be comfortable, but you could survive it. You have both gills and lungs."

"Do you think Theo will survive?" I asked with a smirk, totally kidding.

He laughed and shook his head. "She'll be drinking at my bar every single night, there's no doubt, but that overly dramatic mage will survive you being gone for a week. Besides, you'll still have phones to contact each other, remember? Ain't like the old days when I'd be separated from friends and family for a month on a mission with no contact."

"Do you ever miss the older days?" I asked. Silver rarely talked about his past and I was incredibly curious about it.

He folded his arms across the board one above mine, being so much taller than me, and grunted. "There are lots of things I'd like to forget about, but there were also a lot of good things and good times, even in bad situations. I loved fighting and I was damn good at it, but losing others was hard." His eyes darkened and he said, "I'm glad I snuffed out the evil that had plagued my homeland before I left, even if I lost part of my tusk and soul to do it."

"Your soul?" What did he mean he lost part of his soul?

"That's a story for another time, Daughter. One that will require me to be drinkin'." He stood and dusted off his clothes. "You're going to be alright and even if things get tough, you've got me and the girls to help pick you back up." He held his hand out to me and I let him pull me to my feet.

I hugged him and kissed his cheek. "Thank you, for taking in this orphaned shark."

He patted my back. "Go on home. No more running from life, you hear?"

I saluted him as I walked backwards. "Yes, sir!"

"You come by tomorrow evening, okay?" he called as he turned and headed towards his bar.

"Drinks on the house?" I challenged back, cupping my hands around my mouth to make sure he heard me.

Several people looked at us, but quickly averted their gazes when they saw my wide grin, revealing my shark teeth.

Silver just waved at me without turning to face me.

That was a yes.

I skipped down the street, humming a song I couldn't remember the lyrics to.

My skipping abruptly halted when I found Theo making out with Tristan out in front of the shop she worked at.

Theo stepped back from Tristan her eyes bright with adoration.

"I think I'm going to puke," I muttered and placed a hand on my stomach.

Theo turned and noticed me; her eyes widened, and she squeaked.

Tristan looked in the direction she was and smiled. "Hey, Kass. What are you up to tonight?"

"Kass, I, uh ..." Theo didn't finish the thought.

I waved my hand at them. "I've got to get home. I can't stomach this discussion right now."

"Kass, he isn't like them!" Theo yelled.

Fury blazed down my spine, but I held myself in check.

Theo was my best friend after all, and it wasn't her fault that she'd been suckered into his charm. Instead of spinning around to yell like I wanted, I simply said, "Ask him about winter last year."

Dropping that bomb, I wrapped my arms around myself and resumed walking home.

Tomorrow, my friend and I would have a long chat.

5

"You want to go on a date with me?" Reed asked.

I nodded and smiled wide. "Yes, why is that so hard to believe? It's been a while and I thought it would be nice if we went out to dinner and watched a movie, just the two of us. What do you think?"

"I can't tonight," he said, rubbing the back of his neck sheepishly. "Tomorrow night?"

"It's a date!" I said with a wink, spun away, and hurried up the stairs to my room so I could change to go see Silver and have the dreaded talk with Theo.

"Who are you getting all dressed up for?" Grant teased.

I spun in a circle like I wore a dress despite only wearing a pair of jeans and a tank top. "I was invited to the King's Gala! Can you believe it?"

He leaned his shoulder against my doorframe. "The king better not be single or thinking about setting you up with the prince."

After applying my eyeliner, I turned, hands clasped

together against my chest and said in a higher than usual voice, "Oh, that would be the perfect dream, wouldn't it? If only I were so lucky."

"You don't believe in luck," he countered.

Skipping over, I tapped the tip of his nose and said, "True."

"Reed looked ... perplexed when he left earlier. What did you say to him?"

"I asked him on a date," I replied honestly, walked to my closet, and pondered over which shirt to wear. I could go out in the tank top, but I wanted a nicer shirt. One I could use to catch a few men during my pool shark escapades to pay for my dinner.

"The maroon one with the v-neck," Grant said from the doorway.

I grabbed the shirt and nodded. "Perfect."

"So, what changed your mood?"

"A guy," I said as I pulled the shirt over my head, then winked at him.

"Kass," he growled.

"Silver gave me some fatherly advice," I answered.

"Oh." His eyes widened a moment before his entire body relaxed. "Good. I'm glad you have him."

"Me too."

"Will you be home late?" he asked.

"I might need a pick up," I said honestly. Who knew how much I would drink tonight.

"Have Tonka or one of the sisters text me and I'll fly right over," he promised, kissed my cheek, and left.

Heading down the street towards Silver's Bar, I looked

around at the other people walking. One of the things I loved about this city was the diversity. Humans, shapeshifters, vampires, ogres, trolls, orcs, and more. And none of them knew that we'd come so close to having a kraken overlord.

"You're all welcome," I mumbled.

Several women in matching rompers waited at the front of the line. One of them had a sash proclaiming she was a bachelorette. They laughed and shifted with excitement as they waited to get let in.

I walked up, ignoring the line, but smiled without showing my teeth at the bachelorette as I bypassed them. They smelled interesting, like something fluffy ... what was it? A rabbit! They smelled like rabbits.

Tonka held up his fist as I approached.

I bumped mine against it. "Evening, Tonka."

"Evening, Kass."

"Wait, she just got here and they're letting her in?" one of the women asked.

"Maybe she's sleeping with the bouncer," another whispered.

I stepped on the other side of the rope, turned, and gave the girls a full smile, showing off my teeth, which made them all pale and still.

Yes, that's right, I'm a predator.

Maneuvering my way around all the people, I made my way to the main bar where Silver was serving drinks.

"Oy," I called to get his attention.

He looked over his shoulder from where he was grabbing glasses. "One sec." He spun the glasses in his hand before setting them down, filling them with ice, then moving them to the counter, pouring a few different things into them, and sticking a straw in each.

"You're getting better at that," I said as he came to stand before me.

"I'm bored in my old age so I'm trying new things that the patrons seem to like," he said. "What do you want tonight?"

"Something strawberry," I said and smiled. "Surprise me."

He quickly made a pink, sparkly drink and set it on the bar top in front of me, but kept a hand on the glass so I couldn't take it. "Did you take my advice?"

I nodded. "I asked him on a date and we're going tomorrow night."

"How'd he react?"

The bachelorette party entered and squeezed their way up to the bar at the other end from where I was. One raised her hand at Silver, but he simply held up a single finger to tell her to wait.

"He seemed shocked," I admitted, "but he agreed."

He nodded. "Good." He released my drink and shooed me. "Theo's upstairs."

I took my drink and squeezed through the packed place, up the stairs, and stood a moment trying to spot her.

The bar was unusually packed tonight, so it took me longer than usual to see her in the back corner in one of the high-backed plus chairs that sat around a thin circular table just big enough for a few drink glasses.

She raised her hand when she saw me and stood out of the chair. Tonight, she wore a flowy tie dye skirt with slits up each thigh and a matching tie dye halter top. Her wig was long, curly, and bright pink, and she'd matched her eyeshadow and lipstick to the wig.

I hugged her before I sat and then we both clinked our glasses against each other.

"You look lovely," I said.

She put her hand against her cheek and batted her eyelashes. "Why, thank you. You look good, too."

"Thanks, Grant picked out the shirt."

"Definitely a good choice."

Never one for swimming around the coral, I blurted out, "I'm going with the guys to a poker tournament in the desert."

Her eyes widened and she blinked slowly a few times as she absorbed what I'd just said. "For how long?"

"A week."

"You're abandoning me here for a full week? Wait, you're going to a desert? Are you going to be able to handle that? Have you ever been away from the ocean? No, of course you haven't."

I shrugged. "It might be my last chance to convince Reed to stay with me."

"Is it really that bad?" she asked softly.

"Let's focus on something else equally important," I said and narrowed my eyes at her. "You and the cor ... dolphin shifter." If they really were dating, I couldn't keep calling him insulting names or that would just drive a wedge between us. It was better to talk to her logically.

Maybe Reed was right and I was too biased from being bullied by them, but it wasn't as if Tristan hadn't done anything wrong. He had been in on the bullying, participating in it, not just standing off to the side.

"I know he did some awful things before, but he's changed a lot recently," she said. "He said he really regrets what he did to you and that he's wanted to apologize, but on land you're stronger than him and he didn't want his arm bitten off."

That would have been a likely outcome.

"We've all done some messed up things and I know you hate dolphin shifters, but he's really nice, treats me well, and makes me happy."

It was really difficult for people to change for good. Many times the change was temporary. For my friend, though, to keep our friendship good and allow her to enjoy the happiness, I would hold my tongue on the matter.

"If he makes you happy, I'll hold my judgment," I said. "However, I'm going to continue watching for red flags and you better listen when I point them out."

Her eyes brightened and she smiled.

"But! If he hurts you, I'm going to bite his arm off," I threatened.

She leaned over the table and hugged me. "I love you."

"I love you, too."

"Hey! Shark bitch!" a deep voice yelled.

Theo and I turned around and looked at the person with a death wish.

It was Preston, Reed's former pack member.

"Fuck," I whispered.

6

Preston, Reed's former pack member, marched towards us with a deep frown.

"Kass?" Theo asked.

"Get Tonka or one of the other bouncers," I said softly. "I don't know what he wants and not sure if this will end in bloodshed or not." It likely would.

Theo hurried down the stairs.

"Can I help you, Preston?" I asked calmly and stood, drink in my hand so I could casually take sips. Rule number one in the predator world, never show fear.

Preston stopped in front of me, towering over me and obviously trying to intimidate me.

It was not working.

He growled. "Did you put a spell or use witchcraft on Reed?"

"I can't use witchcraft," I said honestly. "Why would you think I did that anyway?"

"We offered him everything he's ever wanted, exile

removed and a chance at having a litter. Yet, he hesitates and claims to have some type of connection with you." He said "you" like it was a foul word.

The information he gave me made me smile wide, which incidentally showed off my teeth. "So, you're upset that he might actually like me? You're upset that he might have a pack that was found instead of assigned and he prefers that? Why are you so upset that he found someone who loves him? Just because you want more werewolves to be created?"

"It is his duty to provide—"

I held my hand up. "I'm going to stop you right there. Duty does not exist. It's a made up idea by a society that is too toxic to keep their members organically."

His lip lifted in a snarl.

"I'm not forcing Reed. I'm not begging him not to go. I am allowing him to make his own decisions. I understand that a concept like that is foreign to someone like you, but..." I shrugged one shoulder and took a long drink from my cup.

"Fuck you," he growled and swung his meaty fist at my face.

I dodged the fist, spun away, and took another drink. "You're obviously angry, but you're taking it out on the wrong person. You should be mad at the people who decided to exile Reed in the first place."

Claws grew out of his fingertips and his teeth sharpened into canines.

"Oh, scary," I teased and let my teeth grow larger. "Want to see whose can bite through bone cleaner? Spoiler alert, it's mine."

The other two guys who'd come with him the first night walked up the stairs, taking spots behind me.

"Oh no, they've got me surrounded," I said in a higher-pitched voice and put a hand against my cheek. "I'm so scared."

"You should be," Preston growled and shifted into half-shift. His shirt tore and pieces floated to the floor. His head shifted into a wolf's head and his body was covered in fur.

The other two followed suit.

Where was Theo with the bouncers?

Downing the rest of my drink, I set it on the table that was beside me and winked at the couple cowering there. "Watch that will you?" With a deep breath, I shifted into my half-shift, letting my head become more shark-like, my skin becoming grey with stripes just like in my shark form, and let a bit of my tail grow out as well.

"What the fuck?" one of the two behind me asked.

"What are you?" the other one asked.

I turned and said, "I'm your worst nightmare," then winked. With their wide eyed surprise making them freeze, I spun and hit the two behind me with my tail, sending them sailing over the edge of the banister and down to the first floor where women screamed in surprise.

Preston howled his fury and charged towards me with his claws extended as he prepared to swipe at me.

I ducked and dodged out of the way of his swipes, dancing around the center of the upper floor to try to avoid the patrons who sat in their chairs. "You're pretty slow," I critiqued, "and telegraph your movements with your wide swings."

"If I kill you, Reed will return with us," he said.

An opening came and I punched him in the stomach as hard as I could, knocking him onto his back. He gasped for air for a few beats.

"If you kill me, you won't make it out of this city," I countered. "You're in my father's bar. Threatening me is really stupid right now."

"Enough!" Reed barked as he stomped up the steps to us.

I pointed at Preston and shifted to my human form. "He started it!" I pointed at the couple I set my drink down. "They were witnesses."

They both nodded with eyes wide, clearly terrified.

"What are you thinking?" Reed asked Preston. "You think killing her would make me more compliant?"

"She's bewitched you!" Preston growled.

"You're drunk," Reed said. "Get out of here before I take offense to you threatening the one I'm courting."

"Courting? You're courting that ... monstrosity?"

I stuck my lower lip out in a pout. "But I'm a cute monstrosity."

Reed laughed and pointed at the stairs. "Get out of here, Preston. Don't bother her again or we'll have a duel. You remember what happened last time we dueled?"

Preston flinched, which made me *really* curious about what had happened last time. Without another word, Preston walked down the stairs.

Theo and Silver came up the stairs with smiles.

I put my hands on my hips and narrowed my eyes. "And where were you two? I specifically asked for you to get a bouncer, Theo."

"We were dealing with cleanup downstairs after two werewolves fell from this floor," Silver said. "It took us a minute to get up here."

"Mmhmm," I said with as much disbelief into that sound as I could.

"Are you hurt at all?" Reed asked and set a hand on my cheek.

I looked up and smiled wide. "Nope! Although, my feelings are a little hurt from being called a monstrosity."

He kissed me lightly on the lips and said, "You are a very cute monstrosity."

Was I cute enough to convince him not to leave? That was the most important question.

7

"Choosing is impossible!" I shouted, and stormed down to the living room where Grant, Jong-min, and Jong-hyun watched television.

Packing my suitcase for the trip was frustrating me because I couldn't decide what to bring.

"Are you sure I can't be transported on the plane in my tank?" I asked as I sat on Jong-hyun's lap.

He stroked my hair and purred softly. "Sorry, love, but you cannot bring your tank. Plus, it would be really expensive to take it since we would have to ship you on a cargo plane instead of a normal one. Plus, it could break during transport to and from and then you wouldn't have a tank here and you'd have to save up to buy a new one again. Do you really want to be on a cargo plane in your tank instead of with us?"

"Can you help me pack? I can't decide on clothes," I whispered and leaned my head back against his shoulder.

He kissed my cheek and nodded. "Of course. Do you want to eat first before we tackle it?"

"What time is it?" I asked and realized I had left my cell phone in my bedroom.

"Six o'clock," Jong-min answered.

I jumped up. "Oh no! I have my date with Reed in thirty minutes and I'm not ready!"

Rushing upstairs, I quickly got dressed, did my hair and makeup, and ran back down.

"Don't wait up!" I called as I ran outside.

Luckily, we were meeting at a restaurant nearby, so I didn't have to worry about getting a ride. And, we had made a reservation, even though we were regulars and they likely would have seated us quickly even without one.

A block to the restaurant, I slowed and took deep breaths to calm my heart. It wouldn't do to show up huffing and puffing for our date. He didn't need to know I was almost late.

When I opened the door to the restaurant, it was to find three men with guns aimed at the patrons.

One of them spun and aimed it at me. "Don't move!" he shouted.

I put my hands up and froze, the door hit me in the back since I was partially in the doorway.

"Walk slowly into the restaurant," one of them ordered.

Guns usually meant one thing ... humans. Why were humans in a restaurant with weapons?

"I don't have any money or jewelry," I told them. "So, I'll just back out."

I took all of two steps before one of them shot me.

Women in the restaurant screamed and everyone cowered on the ground with hands over their heads.

Looking down slowly, I stared at the spot the bullet had hit, tearing a hole in my dress, but not able to penetrate my shark scales. "This is my favorite dress!" I snapped as fury consumed me.

"What the fuck are you?" the one who had shot me squeaked.

"I am vengeance," I said in a deep voice. Drawing on my power, I let out more of my scales to protect from the additional bullets they were likely going to shoot at me. Springing forward, I grabbed the gun from the one who had shot me and swung it like a bat to hit him in the head. Bone crunched, blood sprayed, and he fell to the ground.

The other two snapped out of their surprise and started shooting. Some humans were stupid and these two seemed really stupid, so I ran between them. Just as expected, they continued firing, aiming at me, and ended up shooting each other as I ran between them.

Both men fell and the restaurant became silent.

"Kass!" Reed yelled as he ran inside, likely having heard the gunfire from outside. He jumped over the dead human and grabbed my arms. "Are you okay?"

My teeth ached to tear into flesh. Killing them in this way wasn't satisfying at all. I should have bitten their heads off while they screamed and begged for mercy. I should have torn an arm off or ...

"Kass," Reed said again and set his hand on my cheek.

Shaking my head to clear the bloodlust, I let my body shift back to human and dropped my head against his shoulder. "They shot a hole in my favorite dress."

He pushed me back and examined the hole on my stomach and pressed down, likely looking for blood.

"No injuries," I said. "Just upset." I looked around the room at the patrons starting to get to their feet. "Is everyone else okay?"

I hadn't realized that the same bachelorette group was here and they immediately rushed over to me, crying. "Thank you for saving us," the bachelorette cried. "I thought I was going to die before I ever got married!"

I patted her head awkwardly. "You're okay now."

"Thank you," the others in her party chorused and took turns hugging me.

Reed smiled as he watched my awkwardness and embarrassment. I was never the savior or the one praised. I was the villain or seen as evil in most situations. It was ... weird.

"We have to close for tonight, but please come back tomorrow and your food will be on the house," the restaurant manager said, teary-eyed, as he shook my hand vigorously.

"Okay," I agreed, not one to turn down free food.

The police came a short while later, took everyone's statements, and the surveillance videos for proof.

"Well, since this place isn't open now, where else would you like to eat?" Reed asked, his arm around my waist.

"Tacos," I said. "I want tacos."

He nodded. "Okay, let's get tacos." We walked in silence a bit as we headed to our favorite taco place and I finally felt the bloodlust fully dissipate. "Are you really okay?" he asked. "I'm sorry I was late. I should have been there sooner."

"If you'd been there sooner, you might have gotten shot

instead of me and you don't have bulletproof skin, Reed. I'm really okay."

He shook his head and growled. "I'm sorry."

I set my hand on his forearm, stopping him just outside of our favorite Mexican restaurant. "Reed, you really don't—"

His arms wrapped around me and he hugged me tight, burying his head against my neck. "I know you're capable of protecting yourself. I know you aren't a damsel in distress. That doesn't mean that I shouldn't protect you. I'm courting you and that means I should do everything in my power to protect you. Knowing you were shot, that you could have been killed, sets off my protective instincts. If you hadn't used your scales, or been too slow to use them, I could have walked into that restaurant to find you bleeding on the ground." His grip tightened and I was glad for my strong skin or I might have had to ask him to release me. Instead, I relished the tightness, the closeness I'd been missing for so long.

"You weren't there to protect me," I reminded him. "Are you going to blame yourself if I'm injured when you aren't here in the future? That'll lead to insanity. Let's just focus on the fact that I'm uninjured and enjoy our night, okay? The only important thing is to focus on our now, not the uncertainty of the future or what-ifs."

He leaned back and looked down into my eyes. "Kass..."

Whatever he'd been about to say was interrupted by a group of drunk males shouting and laughing as they walked by.

"Let's get some tacos," I said with a smile, kissed his cheek, and linked our hands together.

He returned my smile and said, "Tacos *and* margaritas."

My smile widened. "You know the way to my heart."

Once seated and margaritas before us, I told him about the stupid humans I'd defeated.

He relaxed and laughed as I told him about it and things finally felt like they were going back to normal between us.

He told me about work and I told him about some of the kids who'd come to see me.

"You know, you're getting quite famous for your aerobatics in the tank," he said with a smirk.

My eyebrows rose. "I am?"

He nodded. "Lot of kids are talking about it and there's even a discussion board questioning the oddness of it since sharks don't normally do backflips. Some think you're a super intelligent shark. Some have mentioned you possibly being a shifter, but overall, everyone seems to love that you are part of the aquarium, so you don't have a reason to worry. So long as you don't shift, I think you're just making little kids excited to see you and come to the aquarium."

I felt my cheeks warm and looked down at my drink. "I love seeing their smiling faces. When I first started, they looked at me with awe, but also fear and I didn't like that fear. That's when I started doing it. I just hope I don't end up getting the aquarium in trouble if someone does discover I'm a shifter."

He set his hand on top of mine on the table and when I looked up, he smiled warmly at me, so handsome and loving. "You're doing good not just for the kids, but your species. There are kids now doing projects and research on tiger sharks, a species not previously discussed frequently. I think it's awesome. You're awesome."

Warmth bloomed in my chest, but there was still that bit of coldness, fear, that he was going to ultimately leave me.

"Thank you," I whispered and looked down so he wouldn't see that sour note on my face. So I wouldn't ruin our date, which had been awesome so far.

We finished our meals and drinks, then strolled down the city streets, hand in hand. I swung our arms a little bit, smiling like a kid headed to a candy store.

"Would you like to head home and watch a movie?" he asked. "I can make caramel popcorn."

My eyes widened. "Yes, please!" I said excitedly. "I haven't had your famous caramel popcorn in a long time. I've been dying to have some."

"Well, let's hurry home then," he said, picked me up, and started running down the street. People shouted in shock as he flew by them while I laughed giddily.

Once at home, he set me down to open the door, but I grabbed the front of his shirt and pushed him against the door, pressing my lips against his at the same time.

His hands dropped to my hips and he kissed me back, his lips and tongue just as aggressive as mine.

My hand fumbled behind me to open the door and we both nearly fell as we shuffled inside. He kicked the door closed and steered me into the living room, which was thankfully empty, gently lowering me to the couch and pressing himself atop me, his lips never leaving mine.

His hands pushed up the hem of my dress and when I sat up, he tore it off completely.

I pouted, but he said, "I'll buy you a new one."

Tugging at his shirt, he tore it as well. I smirked and said, "I'll buy you a new one."

We laughed softly and he rested his hand against my cheek. "You're so beautiful, especially when you laugh."

"Serrated teeth and all?" I asked.

He nodded. "Serrated teeth and all." His lips crashed into mine and with his hot, smooth skin against mine, I lost all train of thought after that.

8

Morning sunlight broke through the curtains, waking me where I lay, naked and sprawled across Reed.

"Well, you two clearly had a good night," Grant commented as he walked into the room drinking a cup of steaming coffee.

"What time is it?" I asked around a yawn.

"Time for you to get ready for work," Grant answered, "or I would have let you two continue sleeping."

I nodded, kissed the still sleeping Reed on the cheek, stood, and kissed Grant as I walked by.

He slapped my bare butt and winked at me when I looked back. "Couldn't resist."

Rolling my eyes, I skipped up the stairs to take a quick shower and dress.

Today was the last day of work before we left for the tournament, so I was going to put on my best performance yet. The aquarium was going to put a sign up that I was sick and would return soon, which I hoped wouldn't worry the kids too much.

When I made it to the kitchen, Grant had a breakfast sandwich wrapped in a paper towel waiting for me, as well as an energy drink I'd recently found that I loved the taste of.

Reed shuffled into the kitchen, still half asleep, but his eyes brightened when he saw me. He walked over and pulled me into a hug, claiming my mouth with a deep, hungry kiss that had me wishing we could stay home instead. "Good morning, beautiful."

The bond between us thrummed and, had I been feline, I would have purred. "Good morning, handsome."

Grant held out a metal travel mug towards Reed. "Your coffee."

Reed took it, grabbed a breakfast sandwich from the table, and headed towards the door.

"Did you turn him into a zombie?" Grant teased.

I grabbed my breakfast, took a bite, and said, "No comment."

Grant chuckled and slipped his arm around my waist as we headed to the car. "Well, you're welcome to do the same to me tonight."

Swallowing my bite, I answered, "Can't. Tonight is trivia night."

In the Fall, when there were less tourists, Gina offered a weekly trivia night at her pizza place. Theo and I went as often as we could, enjoying being one of the top teams.

"Oh, right," he said with a soft exhale. "Guess we'll order in and watch something."

"Why don't you all come?" I asked. Normally, it was just Theo and I, but there was no reason they couldn't come, too.

"You want us to come?" he asked, stopping at the car to look down at me.

I nodded. "Yeah. You guys can form your own teams and compete against us. It'll be fun. While I do enjoy times out with just Theo, I also always enjoy you being with me, and the trivia nights aren't just Theo and I hanging out, but lots of our friends show up, too. So, it wouldn't be abnormal for you guys to be there as well."

The truth was, with this recent development with Reed, I wanted to spend as much time as possible with them, in case they all did end up leaving.

Grant pressed his fingertips against my chest, a scowl on his face, and whispered, "I can sense your fear, sweetheart."

Swallowing the feelings down, I smiled wide and said, "Well, you guys can decide if you want to come or not. No pressure." Before he could say anything else, I climbed into the backseat and focused on consuming my breakfast.

Grant took a minute to get into the car, during which Reed glanced at me in question, but I didn't reply.

Once at the aquarium, I hurried to the locker area located behind the tanks, where I could strip and climb into the tank without anyone seeing me, that also had access to the large tank the kids came to see me at.

As I swam out into the large tank, joining the sea creatures there, I felt an uneasiness in my chest.

This trip was going to be my last chance to really show Reed what it would be like to be with me, to be fully mated to me.

It would also be my first trip with the others, so I wanted to make sure we all had fun and there were no regrets later.

Most of the fish and the sea turtles veered away from me far more than normal.

Swimming around the perimeter of the circular tank, I let my shark brain take over to stop focusing on my fears and worry, which were obviously being sensed by the others in the tank.

An hour later, the first group of students entered, pressing up against the glass to get a better view of everything in the huge tank.

Among the children was the little girl with the pink bow who came at least once a month to see me with her mother. Today, she held a stuffed creature, it took me a moment to realize it was a tiger shark. She was holding ... me.

Spinning in joy, I did a barrel roll in the water that had everyone squealing and exclaiming in excitement.

The little girl hugged her shark tighter as her smile grew for me.

I knew I couldn't do too much out of the ordinary for them or I really would risk exposing myself, but throughout the day, I did several more rolls and spins, especially when the parents weren't looking.

All too soon, the day ended and I climbed out of the tank. Looking back at it forlornly, I tried to tell myself it was only for a week, but it felt like I was seeing it for my final time.

"Great work today," Stacy, the manager, waved at me. She was a tall, thin woman who loved wearing business suits. Today, her platinum blonde hair was in a high, tight bun, and per usual, not a single hair was out of place. Her teal eyes sparkled like she'd sprinkled glitter inside them.

"Thanks," I said and smiled at her as I pulled on my pants. "I saw a little girl with a tiger shark plushie. Did you guys start selling them?"

She smirked and held out a small manila envelope. "That's part of why I came to see you."

"What's this?" I asked, opening the envelope.

"Your popularity has risen so much that we started offering merchandise. We felt it was only right to offer you a portion of the proceeds."

My eyes widened at the check and the amount listed there. "Th-This is for me?"

She nodded. "You can thank the girl with her little pink bows. She demanded to know where Kass's items were in the shop and asked every single time she came."

"C-Can I see the items?"

She held up a small tote bag I hadn't noticed at her side. "I grabbed you one of each item."

Tears welled in my eyes as I looked inside the bag at the plushie, pins, magnets, and t-shirts.

"Don't worry about you being gone, either. We're going to let them know that you're sick, but not to worry at all because the doctors are handling it and you'll be back for them to see just as soon as you're one hundred percent better."

"Thank you, Stacy." She had given me a chance, provided me a job, and previously a place to sleep. It was a lot of give someone you barely knew.

"Girl, I should be giving you twice that check. You've brought in tons of business and a lot of social media presence.

Your aerobatics is so widely discussed that people are flying in from out of state just to try to see your antics."

"Aren't you worried someone might question my true form?" I asked, looking into her eyes.

She shrugged a shoulder. "Technically, we aren't breaking any laws by having you swim around. Bars have mermaids who do the same types of 'shows' and you're on our books, so it's not like we aren't reporting your wages. The laws are in place to protect shifters and you aren't a captive here. We'll be fine even if we have to announce it, but we don't plan to."

"I'd rather the kids think I'm just a smart creature," I admitted softly.

Her smile softened and she nodded once. "I understand your wishes and will try my best to continue following them. Now, get on out of here! You've got to finish packing still, if I know you well enough."

Cringing, I nodded. "You're right. Thank you, again, for everything."

She waved. "Just make sure you come back, okay? I don't want to lose my star."

Hugging the envelope and tote to my chest, I sniffled and walked out of the aquarium feeling so happy I wanted to cry.

"What's wrong?" Reed asked and growled softly. "Whose ass do I need to kick?"

That had me laughing and a few tears leaked out. I wiped them away and kissed his cheek. "Happy tears, handsome. Happy tears."

He draped an arm around my shoulders and steered me

towards the car. "Oh, well, in that case. Yay, whatever made you happy."

I shook my head and said, "Thanks."

Grant waved from where he leaned against the car. "Ready to finish packing?"

"Nope, but I've put it off long enough. I'll just grab the first outfits that draw my eyes and force myself to be happy with what I bring when we are there."

"You could walk around naked, with your scales as an outfit, and no one would care," Reed said.

"I definitely wouldn't mind it," Grant said and had to adjust his pants.

Throwing my head back, I laughed loudly. This was how they'd wormed their way into my hearts. Laughter and love. I just hoped they stayed there.

9

"I should have lied and said I couldn't shift my tail so we could have gotten seats with more leg room," I complained as we sat in our seats on the crowded plane.

Reed raised the arm rest between he and I up so he could reach over comfortably and set his hand on my thigh. "It's not a very long flight, only an hour and a half. You'll survive."

"It's not like you're very tall anyway," Grant commented on my other side and raised the arm rest between us as well, setting his hand on top of his thigh, palm up, fingers spread in invitation.

I accepted and threaded our fingers together. The touch of both of them helped relax me and I closed my eyes with an exhausted sigh.

I hadn't been able to sleep well due to the anticipation of our trip.

The flight attendants gave their preflight speeches, describing all the features of the plane, emergency exits, and things to do in case of emergency.

They were not instilling confidence in me.

"Flying really isn't that bad once you get used to it," Grant said softly and leaned closer to me, rubbing our shoulders together. "The sooner you get used to it, the sooner we can take you on more trips, ones even farther from here."

"More trips?" I asked, opening my eyes and looking at him.

He smiled and nodded enthusiastically. "There are so many places I want to show you. So many fun cities that I know you would enjoy visiting. Also, other countries."

Other countries? I had been to several, but had gotten there by swimming.

"Maybe we could take a ship," I suggested.

"Ships take too long," Grant grunted. "You'd get there much faster on a plane."

The plane started moving and I squeaked in fear.

A small child sitting with his parents across the aisle snickered at my fear.

I leaned forward and stuck my tongue out at him, which he did back, earning me a scowl from his uptight father. Judging by the pointed ears and long, straight hair, they were likely elves. Elves were often super uptight, so all things fit. Not that I didn't like elves, but they weren't exactly party people. I'd learned quickly not to try to use my pool shark scam on them. They were grumpy when swindled.

"You sure you don't want kids?" Grant asked softly. "You have a super soft spot for kids."

I leaned back and closed my eyes with a scowl. "No. I just want to be someone's crazy aunt."

He was right, I did love kids, but I didn't want the responsibility of children or possibly giving them whatever curse I had. Okay, I wasn't cursed, anymore, but I still didn't feel right bringing a child into the world as it was. As I was.

"You'd look super cute all round and pregnant with our pups," Reed whispered in my ear with a growl, his hand sliding higher up my thigh and squeezing slightly.

Desire rolled through me and I exhaled shakily.

"Sir, do you want to get us kicked off this plane?" I asked without looking at him.

He chuckled softly and left me alone, releasing his grip and letting his hand slide back down to just above my knee.

The attendants passed out snacks and Grant ordered drinks for us.

I gladly accepted mine, downing it in one gulp before devouring the snacks, mostly pretzels, as well. My stomach was nowhere near satisfied.

"Don't worry, we'll be getting dinner as soon as we check into the hotel," Reed said and patted my knee.

"I didn't say anything," I whispered and looked over at him with a scowl. How had he known I was still hungry? He wasn't even looking at me.

His brows furrowed and he opened his eyes, blinking up at the plane's ceiling. "I, uh, felt it," he whispered.

"You *felt* my hunger?" I asked in a hushed voice, so as not to draw attention to us. "Is it because of our ... unique bond?" We hadn't really talked about it, but he, Grant, and I had developed a unique bond that first night we'd spent together. When they'd started courting me, it had only gotten stronger.

He closed his eyes, scowling hard. "I don't know, but it's best not to think about it."

His glib response hurt so much that I inhaled sharply and had to turn my face away as tears burned at the back of my eyes.

Of course he wouldn't want to think about our connection. If he did that, he might have to admit that there was more to us than a normal relationship and that would sway his decision on whether to return to his clan or not.

Grant squeezed my hand and I leaned over against him, rubbing my face against his shoulder to stop the tears from coming and to ease the tension I felt by inhaling his scent.

He kissed the top of my head softly, let go of my hand, and slid his arm around my shoulders to pull me closer into him, forcing my head to rest on his chest.

Closing my eyes, I focused on the beat of his heart and let it drown out everything else.

Everything else except the pain that seemed to beat in time with his heart.

IO

"It's so big!" I exclaimed as I looked up at the hotel with well over fifty stories.

"That's what she said," Grant said with a laugh.

Jong-min groaned and shook his head. "I expect it from her, but now you, too?"

"Hey!" I turned and glared at him. "You're not supposed to be rude to me on this trip, remember?"

He shook his head. "I made no such agreement."

As he walked by, I pinched his butt, earning a growl from him, which made me smile wide.

I stepped through the revolving doors and into the lobby of the luxurious hotel. The high ceilings and wide-open floor plan made it seem even larger than it was. There were plush carpets and elegant chandeliers hanging from the ceiling. The walls were adorned with large paintings and sculptures, creating a sophisticated atmosphere. In the center of the lobby was a large, ornate desk where a concierge was assisting a couple checking in. Behind the desk was a wall of windows that allowed natural light to flood the room, illuminating everything in a warm glow.

To my right, a group of businessmen were gathered in one of the many seating areas, discussing the day's meetings over coffee. To my right, a couple was relaxing on plush couches, cuddling together as they sipped on their drinks.

Throughout the lobby, hotel staff bustled about, attending to guests' needs and ensuring that everything was in order. I could hear the hum of activity, the low murmur of conversations, and the gentle sounds of classical music playing softly in the background.

"Let's hurry and check in so we can drop our suitcases off," Reed said and walked to get in line.

He hadn't said two words to me since the comment on the plane. I had to find a way to break the ice and get us back to where we were after our date.

I hated that I had to suck it up and act like nothing had happened when I was in pain, but it was for the best.

Skipping over to join him in line, I put my arms around his waist and squeezed. "What are we going to have for dinner?"

He looked down at me and a half smile appeared. "What would you like? There's almost every type of food here that you could think of."

"Um, you pick. I'll eat anything," I said and shrugged my shoulders.

"We can go to one of my favorite restaurants, it's just a block away, and you'll definitely love the food," he said with a smile.

I leaned my head against his shoulder and tightened my grip around his waist. "Sounds great."

It was finally our turn to check in, but instead of going with him, I walked back to the others.

"How do you feel about going to a club tonight?" Grant asked.

"A club?" I asked and looked up at him.

"Yeah, dancing and drinking." He smirked. "The twins love clubs."

Looking over at the scowling Jong-min, I couldn't see it. "Um, okay." I would love to see the twins enjoying themselves, so going to a club to get them to dance sounded super fun.

"We're checked in," Reed said as he rejoined us with five keycards in his hand. "Fortieth floor."

I swallowed hard and followed them towards the elevators. "That's ... high."

"You'll be fine," Jong-hyun said and slipped an arm around my waist, pulling me so our hips pressed together while we stood in the elevator.

The elevator started moving up and I inhaled sharply at the disorienting feeling. "Sharks don't like heights that don't involve water. You're fine with it because cats always land on their feet."

Jong-min chuckled behind me.

"Perhaps you just need to work on your balance then," Jong-hyun whispered. "Do not worry, love, we will catch you if you fall."

Would they be there to catch me if I fell if Reed left?

"What are our room arrangements?" I asked to rid myself of that thought.

"Well, we figured you would probably flit between our beds and not need your own," Grant said. "So, we have two adjoining rooms with two beds each. Reed and I are sharing one room and the twins are sharing the other room."

"Sounds good to me," I replied with a wide smile.

Our rooms were really nice with a great view of the city. Being so high up gave me almost instant vertigo, though, so I didn't get right up to the windows to look out.

I fell down onto the bed Jong-min had chosen and rolled onto my side to look out the windows they'd opened the curtains on.

He sat down beside me on the bed, silent for a bit before he finally reached over and smoothed some hair back from my face. "You've been awfully troubled lately. Do you want to talk about it?"

"Not much to say," I whispered back, not wanting Reed to hear. "It's not up to me at this point."

He ran a hand up and down my arm, soothing me a bit with his touch. The male may have been grumpy often, but I knew he truly cared for me. "We are here for you and aren't going anywhere."

"You don't know that for sure," I whispered back, tears building in my eyes. I quickly blinked them away and sat up. "How are my parents doing? You've been staying late to help them with more than just the restaurant, haven't you?"

He nodded and looked down at his hands in his lap. "They are getting older, less able to complete tasks they normally would. We are helping them as much as we can."

I set my hand on top of his. "Thank you. That's something that's been weighing on my mind, so I appreciate that you two have stepped up to help them. It should really be me helping them."

"They are pushing us to complete our bonds," Jong-hyun said. "Very pushy."

I laughed and shook my head. "Mother never thought I'd find someone, so I think she wants to ensure she sees me fully bonded before ... you know." I didn't want to even say it, just thinking about them not being around anymore hurt. I may not see them often, but they were always in my thoughts. I needed to go visit them more.

"They have threatened us in a variety of ways," Jong-min said.

"Each more creative than the last," Jong-hyun said.

"Threatened you?" I asked and looked up at them.

"They've heard about ... his indecision and they are worried about you," Jong-min answered.

"Please don't let their threats sway you," I said, eyes wide. Mother might be able to curse them, but I didn't think she would. I hoped ...

He smiled and leaned forward to rub our noses together. "Silly woman, we won't."

Pressing forward, I kissed him on the lips.

He responded, wrapping his arms around me as he kissed me back. His hands slid up my back, rubbing and soothing at the same time they excited me.

"Dinner time," Reed announced as he walked into the room through the open adjoining door.

Jong-min leaned back and smiled at me. "Yes, we should feed the piranha. Her stomach is growling very loud."

It wasn't just my stomach that was hungry.

"Food would be good," I said and licked my lips.

Jong-min smirked, the cocky bastard, and kissed my cheek. "Later you can have other desserts," he said, stood, and walked towards the door.

Tease!

II

The restaurant they took me to was swanky with low lighting, velvet curtains along the walls, deep, recessed booths with high walls so you didn't have to see other patrons, and soft instrumental music playing to keep noise down so you didn't overhear others.

They had insisted I sit in the center of the u-shaped booth, Jong-min and Jong-hyun taking the spots on either side of me and Reed and Grant taking the end seats.

I nearly choked on my own spit when I read the prices of just the appetizers.

Setting the menu down, I smiled at Reed and said, "I'll just let you order for me since everything on the menu looks good."

He returned my smile and set his menu down as well. "I can do that."

Grant waved down our waiter and ordered our drinks, getting me a margarita.

"So, tomorrow is the start of the tournament?" I asked.

They all nodded.

"We'll check in around noon and the first game is set to start around two o'clock," Reed answered.

Our drinks came, interrupting him, and I was surprised by the quickness. Was that common at high-end restaurants?

We clinked our glasses together and sat in silence for a little bit as we enjoyed the drinks. It was nice just to be together and relaxed like this. It had been far too long.

The waiter returned just long enough to set down bread and butter.

Jong-hyun quickly buttered a piece for me, then Jong-min, and then himself.

"This bread is really good," I commented as I ate it.

"Everything here is good," Grant said. "It's our favorite place when we're in town."

"Are you guys nervous about tomorrow?" I asked as I ate another piece of bread that Jong-hyun had buttered for me.

"Not really," Reed answered. "We've been practicing and helping each other to ensure we don't have any tells or anything."

"Do they have telepaths monitor the event to make sure no one is cheating?" When I'd found out that they were playing in the tournament I had done a little bit of research and learned that some competitions hired telepaths to listen in on people's thoughts to make sure no one was using their powers to cheat. It made sense in our world of supernatural life.

Reed tilted his head to the side a bit as he looked at me. "They do. How did you know about it?"

I leaned back with my drink in my hand and smiled. "I did some research."

"You researched poker?" Jong-min asked.

"When I realized my boyfriends had it as a hobby; yes, I did. You know, you guys don't really share your hobbies with me." It was a realization I'd come to when listening in on another couple's conversation at Silver's one night. Most people had hobbies and even if their significant other didn't participate in them, they knew about it.

The guys knew about my pool shark hobby and often participated. I knew they all liked videogames and we played together, but I didn't know about any other true hobbies. Their penchant for outdoor games like volleyball didn't really count.

Part of the problem was how busy we had all been and there hadn't been time for hobbies, not even pool sharking.

"I like to paint," Jong-hyun answered while the others just stared at me like I'd grown a second head.

"Really?" I asked and turned to face him. "How come I've never seen you paint?"

"Too busy lately," he said and shrugged. "We could do a group painting where I teach you guys each step and we paint together."

I nodded with a wide smile. "That sounds awesome!"

"Have you never painted before?" Jong-min asked.

Spinning on the seat, I turned to face him. "Um, no. Is that weird?"

"I think our scowling partner here just hadn't thought about how many things we consider normal that you may not have experienced due to your life in the sea," Grant said with a soft smile. "Perhaps we should make a list and we can start doing a weekly or bi-weekly date night to teach you?"

"Yes, please!" I shouted a bit too loudly. Putting my hand over my mouth, I laughed softly.

"What do you like to do?" I asked Jong-min.

"I still write songs and sing," he said.

"Still?"

"Pop stars, remember?" Grant reminded me.

"Oh, that's right. You guys still haven't told me what you were called or let me listen."

"I haven't recorded any of my new songs," Jong-min said like that explained it.

"Here," Reed said and handed me his cell phone.

I took it and my mouth dropped as I looked at the picture of Jong-min and Jong-hyun on stage with what definitely looked like makeup on their faces, hair styled to perfection, and a huge crowd before them. "I've heard of you guys!" They were a hugely popular duo that had taken not just their country by storm, but the world. Women were so obsessed with them that they had followed them around the world on their tours, just trying to get a chance to talk to them. One day they'd just quit doing it and no one knew why.

I had a feeling that now was not the time to ask them about why they'd quit though. I didn't want to bring up something that would dampen the mood.

"Wow, I bet a ton of girls would lose their minds if they found out I'm with you," I said and chuckled softly.

"Yes, you are very lucky," Jong-min said with absolutely no shame.

"What about you?" I asked Grant. "What hobby do you have?"

"I don't really have one right now," he said and shrugged one shoulder. "I've done a lot of things over the years, but haven't had a single hobby stick that I liked so much."

"Maybe we could try new ones together," I offered. "Since I don't have a hobby either."

"Pool sharking isn't a hobby?" Reed teased.

"No, that's a business," I said and smiled.

He returned my smile and laughed while shaking his head. "Incorrigible."

"You could start a jewelry business that involves shark teeth, since yours grow back indefinitely," Jong-min suggested. "Lots of humans like shark teeth and shark teeth jewelry."

"You could even have Theo enchant them to sell for more as an enchanted protection charm. I bet they'd sell well," Jong-hyun added.

That was ... a good idea.

"Maybe," I said, "but I don't know if I can create jewelry well. I'll have to try it."

"We can help," Jong-hyun offered immediately. "I made jewelry with my mother a lot when I was young."

"Your jewelry was always wonky," Jong-min said with a scoff. "I will teach you."

"It's a date!" I said excitedly. "We can do that when we return from our trip."

"Reed hasn't told you his hobby yet," Grant commented.

All of us turned to look at Reed who was staring deeply

into his glass of whiskey. Was it my imagination or were his cheeks flushed? Was he embarrassed?

"I haven't done it in a long time," he said softly. "But I like to create furniture."

"Like modeling it or building it?" I asked.

"Building it," he answered. "I like to take driftwood or wood that's been tossed to the side and repurpose it into something beautiful."

Why on earth would he be embarrassed about that?

"That sounds awesome," I said.

"He's really good, too," Jong-hyun praised. "He took some driftwood and colored epoxy and some enchantments and made a gorgeous coffee table."

Jong-min tsked, which made Jong-hyun flinch.

Grant's face fell and Reed suddenly shot to his feet.

"I'm going to the bathroom, I'll be back," Reed said as he hurried away from the table.

"What was that about?" I asked our silent group.

"He'd made that coffee table for his mother. He finished it and the next day was when she stood by the alpha and they banished him," Grant explained. "He put the table in their courtyard, set it on fire, and walked away while she'd cried."

Oh.

12

When Reed had returned to our table, he'd acted like nothing was wrong, which was good, but also worrying. Pushing his feelings down too much would lead to an explosion.

Yes, I knew from experience.

The twins cuddled me extra hard when we finally returned to the room after dinner. I lay between them on the bed, their heat surrounding me and their purrs filling the night.

They were both sound asleep, still not able to handle their liquor very well.

I, however, couldn't sleep. My chest hurt and I wanted to go for a swim, but we weren't home, we were in a desert, devoid of water.

For over an hour I tried to let the twins' purrs lull me to sleep, but that was not in the cards tonight.

Extricating myself from between them, I leaned my head through the open doorway between the shared rooms and saw Grant was still awake. He leaned back against the headboard, his phone in his hand as he scrolled through something.

I tiptoed into the room to avoid waking Reed and crawled up the middle of Grant's bed.

He set his phone down on the side table and opened his arms and spread his legs a little wider so I had room to lay down against his chest with my legs between his. "Can't sleep?" he asked softly and stroked my hair.

"No," I whispered and rubbed my face against his shirtless chest. He smelled so good. Like a campfire. "What about you?"

"Same. I may have lied a little bit when I said I wasn't nervous about the tournament."

I chuckled softly and looked up at him. "You'll do great. I'm sure of it."

He set his hand against the side of my face and rubbed my cheek with his thumb. "You're so beautiful." Leaning forward, he pressed a soft kiss to my lips.

"Do you want to sneak out?" I asked.

"Sneak out?" he asked and arched a brow.

"Well, I didn't get dessert and I saw that the place downstairs has cheesecake slices for sale."

"Sold," he said as he put a shirt on, and we both quickly and quietly slid sandals on, and exited the room.

We waited for the elevator hand in hand, smiling at each other like we were naughty kids on our way to do something we weren't supposed to. The elevator arrived and it was empty as we climbed on and hit the button for the ground floor.

He pushed me against the wall of the elevator and kissed

me deeply, his hands gripping my hips and my hands grip-ping his shirt. Someone got into the elevator on the next floor, but Grant didn't stop kissing me, blocking me from view of the other person with his body.

We finally made it to the ground floor and only then did he stop kissing me.

Swinging our joined hands as we walked, we smiled at each other and ignored anyone around us.

At the display counter, I squatted down and debated for a minute about which cheesecake to get, but finally decided on the strawberry.

Grant got the caramel and chocolate one and we took our desserts over to one of the small booths in the seating area.

"Delicious," I said around my bite.

"Try?" he requested and opened his mouth.

I stabbed a forkful and carefully fed it to him. He did the same for me and I felt that pressure and pain in my chest ease.

We watched some of the people walking around, or stum-bling in a lot of cases, as we ate our treats. Grant grabbed us drinks and sat beside me with his arm around my shoulders.

"I'm sorry that we've been so busy lately," he said and squeezed me. "I think planning out the hobby dates will help us ensure that we make time for each other like we should have been this whole time. I hadn't realized how little we were together until we were talking about this trip and what it would be like if you didn't come. We take for granted that we see you at work and that we have drinks together at Silver's. Yes, we are together often, but we aren't really spending quality time together and that's going to change."

"It's not all on you guys," I said. "I've been so set in my ways that I didn't really think about it either. It's that trap that married couples fall into, you know? And I wasn't feeling neglected or anything, but it would be nice to do more things like this. More one on one times, so I can get to know you guys better. It's weird to feel like I know you, to have this connection, but know so little about your past."

"We aren't exactly open books about our pasts, so not your fault." He chuckled mirthlessly. "We've all dealt with some traumatic shit and take for granted that we know each other's, but you don't know."

"You guys know all about my past now," I said and shrugged. "But I don't have as much to tell."

"You sell yourself short a lot, Kass. You're amazing and you saved so many lives all without proper credit."

"Sharks will never be seen as heroes," I said and sighed dramatically. "Yet another curse of my life."

He squeezed me again and kissed the side of my head. "You're a hero in our eyes. We just can't tell you that or it'll go to your head."

I leaned my head against his shoulder and said, "I lived so long convinced I was going to be alone, but then you guys showed up. Now, I'm worried again. I knew it was too good to be true."

He tilted my chin up with his finger and shook his head. "No, Kass. You don't have to worry."

"He's your packmate," I whispered.

"If he chooses to go back to the werewolves, he's not just abandoning you, he's abandoning us, too. We can't go with him there and we aren't going to accept a mate who is assigned. We all left behind archaic families who wanted to do the same thing and we all refused. We agreed that what we wanted was free will, to find the lives we wanted and live them how we wanted."

"Is that why you guys have been so upset with Reed, too?" I asked.

He nodded. "He's hurting our friendships, our pack bond, but we also don't like seeing him hurt you." He gripped my chin between his finger and thumb and said, "No matter what he decides, Jong-hyun, Jong-min, and I aren't going anywhere. You are the one we want to be with and that hasn't changed."

Tears sprung to my eyes, but instead of letting them fall, I kissed him, then lay my head back on his shoulder and watched people with a smile on my face, the bond between Grant and I thrumming strongly.

"There you are," Jong-hyun said sleepily, rubbing the back of his hand against his eyes as he sat beside me. "I got worried when you weren't in bed, but then saw Grant was gone too and thought maybe you'd be down here."

"How'd you know we'd be down here?" I asked.

"You were staring at the cheesecakes with drool practically dripping down your chin as we headed towards the elevators." He took my fork and ate the last bite on my plate. "Oh, that is good."

Reaching over, I set my hand palm up on his leg and he immediately linked our hands.

"Are you still worrying we might leave with Reed?" he asked.

"She was, but I set her straight," Grant answered.

"I just want to make sure that I'm not the reason you're splitting up," I admitted. It was hard to admit, but I knew I had to be open and honest with them, especially right now.

"My sweet flower, we are all very certain of one thing, you are our future. Reed just needs a minute to realize it, but even if he doesn't, you are my future. My brother and I may be total opposites, but you are exactly what we need and want. Have no doubt about that."

"Min said that you have been threatened by Mother. How bad is it?"

He smiled and I could see the adoration in his eyes. "She threatens, but only because she knows we do love you and she wants you happy."

"I should visit her more," I said and looked down at our joined hands.

"She would like that, but she also knows you are busy and they are thankful for us helping. Plus, you do not cook well so you would only cause trouble."

My mouth dropped open as I looked up at him. "I burnt *one* dish! One! She's never forgiven me."

He and Grant laughed, making me relax again.

"Thank you," I said to both of them.

"No, it is us who should be thanking you," Jong-hyun said with a shake of his head. "You leapt into our world and showed us what love is supposed to be. Showed us a future we hadn't truly thought was possible. Thank *you*, Kassidy, for existing."

13

Grant and Jong-hyun chugged energy drinks at breakfast due to our late-night escape that had us returning to the room well after midnight. After dessert, we'd gone for a walk around the casino and they'd explained some of the games to me, extending the relaxing evening and the joy I felt returning to my chest.

Jong-min and Reed seemed irritated that we'd gone out by ourselves without alerting them, but didn't say much aside from a random growl or two, which was honestly their more common response to most things.

Once they got checked in, the guys all grew very serious and quiet. I stayed at Jong-min's side, at his request, as the rest took turns going to play. Jong-min had the latest start and he said it would make him feel better to have me with him. I found that really odd considering the grumpy feline shifter usually just growled at me, but I wasn't going to look a gift cat in the mouth.

"You won't be able to stand near me while I'm playing,"

he explained as it neared his time. "They would be too worried about you cheating. There is a bar with a view of the table I'll be at, so you can sit there, drink, and look pretty."

"Aw, you think I'm pretty?" I teased to lighten the mood.

"Pretty aggravating," he grumbled, but I knew he was only teasing me.

I kissed his cheek and wrapped my arms around his shoulders, giving him a tight squeeze. "I love you, tiger."

He sighed. "I keep telling you that I'm not a tiger."

He did, but it didn't stop me from saying it often to get the wearied sigh from him.

"I'm sorry I snuck out of bed last night," I apologized, since I hadn't had the chance to do so yet.

He set his hand on my forearm across his chest and patted it twice. "It's alright. I understand the occasional need to escape, especially when sleep evades you."

"When we get home, will you sing for me?" I asked.

"If I win my matches today, I will take you to karaoke and sing for you there," he promised.

My mouth dropped and I nodded vigorously. "Yes, please!"

He kissed my cheek and stood. "Go to the bar there, please, so I can see you while I play."

I grabbed his face between my hands, squishing his cheeks and kissed him hard on the lips. "Go get 'em, tiger."

He sighed, but smiled, and shook his head. As he walked away, he said something in his native language that I was beginning to understand was closely related to "what a brat," in English. Someday, I would learn their language.

Heading to the bar he pointed at, I ordered a drink and sat down to watch him play.

The noise in this area was quieter than a normal casino, but that was due to the poker games and people being a bit more respectful.

Two women sat down next to me, chatting animatedly to each other as they ordered a drink. Both wore club dresses that showed a lot of cleavage and barely covered their butts. As I looked at them and compared my own jeans and t-shirt, I wondered if I had underdressed for the occasion.

They noticed me looking at them and smiled.

I returned their smile, with lips closed, and raised my glass in salute.

They did the same and then moved closer.

"Are you here with one of the players?" the one in the red dress asked.

I nodded. "You two?"

The one in the blue dress nodded. "It's our first time."

"It's my first time here, too," I admitted. "My guys have been here before though."

"I'm Lana, this is Tiffany," blue dress introduced.

"Kass," I replied and shook her hand. Her skin was incredibly soft and delicate and as I inhaled, I quickly realized they were human. Definitely needed to keep my teeth away from view.

"Guys?" red dress, Tiffany, asked. "You lucky bitch."

I laughed and nodded. "I am pretty lucky."

"Are you a shifter?" Lana asked.

I nodded.

"That's so cool!" she shouted.

The bartender shushed her and she quickly dropped her head.

"Are your guys shifters, too?" Tiffany asked.

I nodded. "Yep. What about you two?"

"Vampires," they said simultaneously and giggled like it was something that happened often.

My heart beat faster, but I lifted my lips in a smile. "Well, I'd wish you luck, but since my guys are competing against yours, it wouldn't really be true."

They laughed and started talking to each other about someone they saw far away.

I continued sipping on my drink and watching Jong-min. he always looked cool and composed, but playing poker, he was a textbook definition of it. There was still so much for me to learn about these men.

"So, you're the infamous Kassidy, huh?" a woman asked as she sat on my right.

I glanced over at her, but didn't recognize her. She had long, wavy blonde hair, thick lashes that framed brilliant blue eyes, and a fit body shown off in a black bodycon dress. I was definitely underdressed for this event. "Sorry, I don't think we've met."

She flipped her long hair over her shoulder and held her hand up to the bartender, who was at the other end, to get his attention. "No, but I've heard all about you from Preston."

My proverbial hackles were immediately raised. "Preston knows nothing about me," I said, "and you should be careful who you take information from."

"You're a shark shifter, one of the few still alive, and an Atlantean at that, but a banished one. That's probably why

Reed even gave you the time of day, he felt bad for you, just like he feels bad for those other rejects he calls 'pack' ... for now."

"Who are you?" I asked. "And why are you sitting near me like I won't bite your head off, literally, if you don't stop talking poorly about my men?"

The bartender finally came over and she ordered a gin and tonic before turning to face me. "My name is Samantha. I'm Reed's mate."

14

"Assigned mate," I corrected Samantha and finished off my drink. I held up the empty glass to the bartender and he nodded, understanding I wanted a refill.

She shrugged. "Same thing."

"No, it's really not. You see, he *chose* me," I said, feeling extremely defensive and petty.

I barely heard her growl, but her lips twitched in a snarl and I felt it rumble through the bar top where our hands rested. Yep, that made her mad.

"You're keeping him from performing his duty," she said. "Don't you have any conscience?"

"If you really want to get fucked, there are plenty of men around here," I said and waved my hand around at the hundreds of men in our vicinity.

"You're no match for me, *shark*, so just give it up. Tonight, I'm going to convince him to leave you and the pathetic losers he calls friends. So, enjoy your last few hours with him." She tossed money on the bar top, grabbed her drink, and sauntered away.

I did have to admit, she looked good, but I wasn't going down without a fight. Plus, one pretty face wouldn't steal him away. There were lots of gorgeous women in our city that he barely spared a glance for.

Jong-hyun stepped up next to me, scowling. "Who was that? Why are you upset?"

How could he tell I was upset?

"No one of consequence," I said and smiled at him. "Did you win?"

He nodded and ordered a drink before turning to face me, cupping my face in both hands, and rubbing his cheeks against mine. "You sure you're okay?"

"Yes," I answered immediately.

The bartender set our drinks down and Jong-hyun paid for them. "I have to go to another match. Wait here for Min, okay?"

I saluted him. "Yes, sir."

He kissed me lightly on the lips and rubbed the tips of our noses together. "Be careful, but take no crap. You understand?"

My smile widened impossibly large as I looked at my sweet, soft-spoken man and knew he fully supported and accepted me. "You got it."

After he walked away, Tiffany and Lana rushed closer.

"Was that one of your men? Is something wrong?"

"Who was that girl who was glaring at you? She looked angry."

I waved away their concern. "It's okay. Yes, that was one

of my boyfriends. He was just checking on me. That woman was just someone who doesn't like that I've taken so many eligible bachelors out of the dating pool, so she's inconsequential."

"Girl, if all your boyfriends are as hot as that one, I might be mad at you, too," Lana said, and she and Tiffany laughed together.

"Want to do shots?" I asked them, to which I got wide-eyed exuberant nodding.

I caught Jong-min watching me, so I held up my shot, smiled at him, and downed it.

That got me an eye roll, which was better than a worried scowl, so I'd take it.

Samantha thought she could scare me off, but she had no idea the lengths I'd go to for my men. If she wasn't careful, she'd join Koia in losing an arm ... or more.

"How long are you in town? We should do something together," Lana suggested.

"I don't know," I said. "It depends on how well the guys do."

"Well, here's my number," she said and Tiffany wrote hers down as well. "Text us if you want to hang out or do something. We'll even sneak away from our men to go have some girl fun if you want."

Aside from Theo, Zara, and Zyra, I didn't have female friends, so it was a bit odd to have found girls who wanted to be friends this quickly.

"You sure you want to go out with a shark shifter?" I asked and smiled so they could see my teeth.

Both of their mouths dropped open simultaneously and

they asked me at least a dozen questions within five seconds that I couldn't hear all of, let alone answer.

"Yes, these are my shark teeth, no I can't shift them to human shape. It's my one negative as a shark shifter. That's why I usually smile with my lips instead, so I don't scare people. I was worried I'd scare you."

"Scare us? No way! That's so cool," Lana said and leaned forward to look at them better.

"Do you have a special toothbrush for cleaning them?" Tiffany asked.

"Are your boyfriends worried about you biting their you-know-what's off?" Lana asked.

I laughed loudly, earning a glare from the bartender, but I ignored him to answer the girls. "I'm very careful of their you-know-what's, and no, I just use a regular toothbrush."

For the first time, I didn't find it irritating or upsetting to answer a human's questions about my teeth. Was I maturing?

They asked me more questions about my shifting abilities and I answered them all right up until Jong-min finished his game and came over to me.

"Oh my god, you're dating twins?" Lana asked, mouth agape.

"Hot twins," Tiffany breathed.

"Yes, I am," I answered and turned to him. "Congratulations on winning your game."

He dipped his head. "Thank you. Are you ready to get something to eat? You've been drinking quite a bit without consuming any nutrients."

"You could just say you're hungry and know that I'm likely hungry, too," I countered and pouted at him.

He tapped the tip of my nose. "Flower, you are very predictable. Now, let's go before I have to carry you out."

"Text us!" Lana said as I waved to them and let Jong-min lead me away.

Once we were a good distance from them, he turned and asked, "Who was that woman that upset you earlier?"

"The female werewolf who is assigned to be Reed's mate," I answered.

He stopped walking, looked at my face to see if I was being serious, and cussed in two different languages. Immediately, he pulled out his cell phone and sent out a few text messages.

"She's going to try to seduce him tonight," I added.

"She will fail," he growled and stomped towards the restaurant we were meeting the others at.

"Am I prettier than her?" I asked, not actually needing to hear the answer to know he thought I was, or really caring.

"Without question," he said without turning to look at me. "I only noticed her because you were scowling at her and your teeth got longer."

My teeth got longer? He'd noticed that from where he'd been across the room?

"She called you guys losers and it pissed me off," I admitted. "I don't care what she says about me, but her insulting you guys was what upset me."

"The wolves have a habit of talking poorly about anyone who are not wolves. It's part of why I dislike them and was so resistant to Reed in the beginning."

"Well, if she were smart, she'd be trying to win you all over as well instead of alienating his best friends," I said.

"She's clearly not as smart as you," he said.

For some reason, that made me even happier than him telling me I was prettier than her.

"Are you trying to seduce me right now? Because it's totally working," I said breathlessly.

He chuckled, turned around, stopping us at the entrance to the restaurant, and pulled me flush against him. "Tonight, I will show you exactly how I feel about you, since I was unable to do so last night."

"Why tonight? Why not right now, in the bathroom or elevator or hallway."

He smiled, one of his rare true, wide smiles, and kissed me deeply. "When we get back home, I'm going to take you to my favorite location and there, I will make love to you under the stars until you are unable to walk the following day."

"Min, you're not making me any less horny," I said and waved my hand at my face, which was definitely blushing.

"Come, let's eat," he said and tugged me into the restaurant where the others waited for us. "Later will come fun."

15

Grant, Jong-min, and Jong-hyun discussed plans to foil Samantha's seduction attempt that night while we ate dinner. I didn't pay too much attention to them, since I knew Reed wouldn't sleep with her tonight; he wasn't a cheater.

"What if we convince him to get his sperm frozen and give it to her?" I said as I ate my dessert.

Three sets of eyes pivoted to me.

I stopped with my fork in my mouth. "What?"

"Shifters must have a live mating for it to work. They cannot use artificial insemination," Grant explained.

"Really?" I scowled. "That's weird. Must be some stupid magic block. Magic's frustrating sometimes."

"You'd really have been fine with him donating his sperm?" Jong-hyun asked. "That would mean he would have children out in the world."

"Yeah, I understand that he wants to help with the decreasing werewolf population. If I could donate eggs or something to help with the shark population, I would. I just don't fancy the idea of him sleeping with another woman. Giving her a jar of stuff is totally different."

I set my fork down, the discussion ruining my appetite.

Something in my chest tightened and I rubbed a hand against my sternum. What was that? Anxiety? I hadn't felt anything like it before.

The guys resumed talking while I sipped on my drink in silence.

The feeling came again and I pressed hard against my sternum. What was this feeling in my chest? It was a heavy feeling now.

"I've got to go," I said and stood.

They all turned to me with scowls.

"What's wrong?" Grant asked.

I rubbed at my chest and shook my head. "I don't know."

Heading out of the restaurant, hand pressed to my chest, I moved on autopilot. My feet took me to the sitting area by the check in desk. Standing next to the windows was Reed and Samantha. Reed stepped forward and hugged her tenderly, his arms wrapping around her slowly and tightly.

The feeling in my chest increased and from the side of my eye I noticed a gray wispy magical strand. The strand tightened, like a guitar string, and thrummed as Reed leaned back to look down at Samantha's face.

Physical pain and emotional pain burst through me and I felt my body shifting slightly, my teeth elongating and my scales forming along my throat as I continued to stare at them.

I grasped the rope between my hands and pulled it towards my face, my mouth opening.

Reed scowled and started looking around him, but Samantha grabbed his face between her hands and leaned up to kiss him.

"Kass, don't!" Grant yelled and rushed forward.

The urge to bite through the magical strand grew so intense that if I didn't do it, I thought I might explode in pain.

Grant shoved his arm into my mouth, causing me to bite into his arm more than the strand, so only a tiny tear happened to the strand. "Kass, don't," he whispered.

I opened my mouth as wide as I could and stepped back, horror causing my face to fall. "Grant, I ... I didn't mean ... you put your arm. I'm sorry."

He held his arm against his chest and shook his head. "It's not your fault. I'm okay. I'll heal in a minute. Look, it's not even bleeding anymore."

I shook my head hard and suddenly couldn't breathe. My gills opened and closed on my neck, but there was no water for us to breathe. I needed the ocean. I needed water.

"Kass," Reed called, his voice sounded pained.

Samantha tried to hold onto him, but he pulled away from her.

Shaking my head more, I ran towards the exit. I needed to get outside. Out of this box. Away from him.

Outside the hotel in the artificially lit up night, I gasped for breath, but my gills still couldn't work here. There was no water here. This was a desert. A place devoid of water. I was going to suffocate.

Jong-hyun scooped me up into his arms and ran over to a taxi that was waiting to give a ride. He said something to the driver and slid me inside the back, holding me on his lap.

"Breathe with your lungs, Kass. You have lungs for air, but you're panicking. Inhale with your lungs, not your gills."

I shook my head and clutched his shirt. I couldn't. I couldn't breathe.

He pulled out his cell phone and said something in a different language I didn't understand.

Black dots started to crowd in from the corners of my vision.

The taxi swerved around a corner and Jong-hyun leapt out with me in his arms. He ran into a building through a door some stranger held open, down a hallway with the stranger yelling directions behind us, and then dropped me into water.

I flailed for a minute, my brain not comprehending fully what was going on, but my instincts took over and I shifted into my full shark form.

Flicking my tail hard, I propelled myself forward and was finally able to breathe.

After a few full trips around the tank, I realized that Jong-hyun had somehow found an aquarium and I was inside a shark tank.

It took me at least thirty minutes to calm down enough to swim back to where Jong-hyun stood. Peeking the side of my head out of the water so I could look at him with my shark eye, I blinked in question, swimming in smaller circles so I could see and hear him.

He leaned forward on the railing and smiled. "I had worried something might occur to trigger your need for the ocean while we were here. So, I did research to find an aquarium nearby and reached out to a friend who works here to ensure I could get you here no matter the time of day."

The friend in question, the stranger, wiggled his fingers at me, his eyes wide as he looked at me.

I swam in one last circle before shifting back to my human form and reaching up my arms.

Jong-hyun grabbed my hands and lifted me out of the water with ease.

His friend held out a towel for me, eyes averted. "You are a beautiful shark."

"Thank you," I said and patted myself dry.

"You can breathe now, yes?" Jong-hyun asked.

I nodded. "The panic is gone." The pain in my chest had also subsided, but was still throbbing slightly. Touching the center of my chest, I looked up at him. "Is Grant okay?"

"He is perfectly healed, like it never happened."

"What was that?" I asked.

Jong-hyun rested his hand atop mine on my chest and said, "It appears you were going to sever your bond with Reed. Grant stopped you."

Sever my bond? "I-I didn't want to do that. I couldn't really even think. It was just like a need, a necessity to do it." What would have happened if Grant hadn't stopped me?

Jong-hyun squeezed my hand and smiled. "Come, let's get you back to the hotel so you can shower. Your beautiful hair has some kelp in it." He picked out a leaf and tossed it back into the tank.

Turning to his friend, I bowed my head. "Thank you."

"I'm glad I could help."

Jong-hyun picked me up in his arms with the towel still

wrapped around me and carried me out to the taxi that had waited for us.

I cuddled in his lap as we drove and closed my eyes.

Facing Reed after this wasn't going to be easy. I also needed to apologize to Grant again.

The urge to rub my chest was strong, but I didn't dare touch it again now knowing I had almost severed the bond with Reed.

16

Grant had immediately waved away my apology, but had requested I share his bed that night. I accepted and slept wrapped up in his dragon warmth.

Reed didn't come back to the room until after I'd fallen asleep and when I woke up again, he was already gone.

Jong-min was in a terrible mood the next morning, constantly growling beneath his breath. Had he been in feline form, I was certain his fur would have been puffed out.

Instead of going down to the bar to watch their games, I opted to stay in the room and watch television.

The guys argued with me for a bit, obviously worried about me, but all reluctantly left once I agreed to text them if I was going to leave the room.

Eating snacks Grant had gone and gotten for me, I lounged on the couch, nude, and tried to relax.

My cell phone rang and I answered it on speakerphone so I could keep lying on my side and eating chips. "Hello, Theo."

"You haven't called me since you got there," she huffed. "I thought we were friends."

I rolled my eyes at her dramatic-ness. "I'm sorry. Things have been ... interesting."

She paused. "What happened?"

I told her everything that had happened so far and felt tears prickle the corners of my eyes when I finished. Quickly, I wiped them away.

"Do you want me to put a curse on the wolf bitch?" she asked instantly. "I could make all her hair fall out."

I laughed and felt a little of the pressure ease. "I love you."

"I love you, too, and you know I'm serious. I'll curse a bitch faster than you can say, 'tacos.'"

The truth was that I wasn't even mad at Samantha. She was doing what her pack told her to do, following orders she thought were right. In her mind, she was trying to get back what should have been hers all along.

"I'll keep it in mind," I said. "How're things going with you?"

"Tristan and I got into a fight and are sort of broken up right now," she admitted with a sigh. "I don't really even remember how the fight started, but it was a stupid one and we both overreacted."

"I'm sorry. I know you really like him." Even if I didn't like the dolphin, he had made Theo smile a lot.

"Well, I did meet a new guy," she said. "His name is Damien. We've just gone on one date so far, but he's really sweet."

"Is he a shifter, too?" I asked, curious.

"I, uh, actually don't know," she admitted with a soft laugh. "We both have a love of dramadies and spent a lot of our time talking about those instead of ourselves."

"Sounds nice," I admitted.

"Silver misses you," she said quickly. "He's been pouting since you left, but won't admit it's because he's worried about you."

I flinched. "Don't tell him about the incident, okay?"

"Promise." I could just imagine her miming zipping her lips shut.

"How's work? Anymore vampire drama?" Talking with my best friend made the pain and pressure ease until it was barely noticeable. It also made the time fly by and before I knew it, Jong-min and Jong-hyun returned to the room.

They both stopped inside the room when they saw me, naked on the couch surrounded by chips and empty hard seltzer bottles.

"Uh, hi, I, um. I'll clean this up," I said and stood. The bag of chips I'd had fell off the couch and spilled on the floor.

I flinched and bent to start sweeping them inside the bag.

Jong-min sighed while Jong-hyun laughed.

"You are a mess," Jong-min said as he walked over to me.

I thought he was going to help me clean, but he grabbed my shoulders and pulled me up into a standing position. He turned me around, arms still on my shoulders, and pushed me towards the bathroom.

"Where are we going?" I asked.

"Shower," he said. "You have chip dust on you."

I looked down at my chest and noticed a few fingertip smears of chip dust. "Oh."

He turned the water on and yelled, "Hyun!"

Jong-hyun hurried into the bathroom, their travel toiletries case in hand. "Sorry, was grabbing our stuff."

"Wait, are you guys showering with me?" I asked, eyes wide.

Jong-min took off his shirt and pants without replying, his movements enough of an answer.

I watched the delicious twins strip and climbed into the warm water when Jong-min turned towards me.

The standing shower was luckily made for shifters, so the three of us fit easily. I stood beneath the spray, letting the water soak my hair and body.

Hands slipped around my hips to my stomach and pulled me back out of the water.

I blinked away the water, looking over my shoulder at Jong-min.

One of his hands moved down from my stomach, fingers sliding into my folds.

I arched back against his chest and he started purring.

Jong-hyun stepped around us so that he stood facing me, his eyes dark with desire. "You are gorgeous, Kassidy." He kissed my lips and leaned down to take one of my nipples into his mouth.

"You are the most beautiful creature we have ever seen," Jong-min said as he rubbed between my folds, finding my sensitive nub and rubbing it with expertise.

I reached forward and began stroking Jong-hyun's erection. "I'm the luckiest girl in the world," I said as Jong-min pressed his erection against my back. He leaned down and bit my neck gently, flicking his tongue across the bite afterwards.

Jong-hyun switched to the other nipple, reached his arm around my side, and slid his fingers into my dripping core while Jong-min continued to rub me.

My orgasm was so forceful that I screamed.

For once, Jong-min didn't try to quiet me.

"Your next orgasm, you will scream my name," he purred into my ear and pushed my upper back so that I bent forward.

He pushed into me slowly, gripping my hips firmly as he did.

Jong-hyun had stepped back to allow me to bend over, but moved forward now. I eagerly opened my mouth, being extra careful to keep my teeth back as I sucked him in.

He put a hand under my throat and purred, the vibration traveling even into my mouth. "I enjoy feeling myself inside of you."

Jong-min and Jong-hyun stopped talking, their bodies moving in synch as they moved in and out of me.

When my orgasm hit, I couldn't call out anyone's name, but they didn't seem to mind.

At the same time, they both reached forward and cupped one of my breasts as they continued moving.

Jong-min pulled out and spilled his seed down the shower drain with a grunt, a hand on my lower back and the tips of claws digging slightly into my skin.

I thought Jong-hyun would be close as well, but he stepped back and lifted my upper chest so that I stood upright. "I'm not done with you yet."

He pushed my legs apart with his feet and dropped down

to his knees, his mouth closing around my clit and licking hard.

My legs wobbled and I gasped.

Jong-min stepped up to my side and kissed me deeply, his tongue sliding deep into my mouth. Our tongues danced together while Jong-hyun's tongue brought me to orgasm again.

Jong-hyun slid a finger inside of me, pumping quickly while he stroked himself.

Jong-min reached behind me and slid one of his fingers inside as well and they moved at opposite times in and out of me.

I hadn't experienced anything like it before and screamed their names as I orgasmed again and again.

Jong-hyun grunted and bit into my thigh as he found his release.

We stayed in those positions, panting for a bit before they stepped back and smiled matching smiles at me.

"Wow," was all I could say.

"Let's wash you now," Jong-min said. "And then we will take you to dinner."

"Who are you and what have you done with my grumpy cat?" I teased Jong-min.

His expression turned serious and he cupped my face with one hand. "You are all that I want in this world, flower. I may be a grumpy jerk at times, but I want to ensure you know that this, this is what I want."

Jong-hyun rubbed a soap bar over my chest and nodded. "Your happiness is what we value most in this world. We want to ensure we make you happy."

"Oh, I'm very happy right now," I said with a smile. "Though, I'm not sure if my legs will work."

"You just stand there and look pretty while we wash you," Jong-min ordered. "Then we will take you to get nutrients so your legs will work again, and we can try some new things on our bed instead of in the shower."

"Yes, sir," I breathed, already ready for round two.

He clucked his tongue at me. "Later, flower. No need to be so greedy. You have us for eternity."

"Can't blame me for wanting dessert first," I said.

He smiled, one of those rare big smiles, and said, "Thank you for the compliment."

17

The guys ended up in the finals together, which I found extremely entertaining. I sat at the bar again to watch their final match and sipped on a mai tai.

"There you are!" Lana exclaimed as she and Tiffany entered the bar area.

"Hello, again," I said, and smiled at them.

"Oh, your dress is gorgeous," Tiffany complimented.

I'd decided I wanted to dress nice since it was the final game and there was a chance that one of them would win. The dress I'd brought wasn't flashy enough, so Jong-min and Jong-hyun had taken me dress shopping yesterday. Thankfully, this area was big on flashy clothes and it was easy to find a stunning dress. It was low cut, hugged my shape, and sparkled under the lights.

"Thank you," I replied. "I thought I should dress up for the final game." I still wore flip flops, but the dress was long enough no one would see them.

Lana and Tiffany sat on either side of me and ordered drinks.

"I see your twins made it to the final," Lana said.

"Actually, four of the nine players are my boyfriends," I corrected her.

Both of their mouths dropped.

"What?" Tiffany screeched. She looked at the guys and asked, "Which other ones?"

I pointed Grant and Reed out and Grant noticed as I did it, sending me a wink.

"Damn, you are a lucky bitch," Lana said with a laugh.

"And they really don't care about sharing you?" Tiffany asked.

I shook my head. "Nope. They're all friends and this was something they'd planned to do when they formed their group."

Although I was certain they hadn't foreseen ending up with someone like me.

"I'm jealous. My man would flip his lid if I even suggested it," Lana said and pouted.

Chuckling I said, "I hear a lot of humans are staunchly monogamous."

They both nodded.

I shrugged. "Whatever works for you. I honestly thought I'd end up single the rest of my life, so ending up with four is a huge bonus." Or three, depending on how this went. I still hadn't spoken to Reed since the event.

It felt like he was avoiding me, but I also wasn't actively reaching out to him, so I couldn't fault him too much.

Samantha walked in wearing a stunning dress, the front

cut all the way to her belly button and held up with what had to be dress tape. The emerald green color brought out her eyes and looked great with her skin tone. She sat at the other end of the bar, flipping her hair over her shoulder to block me from her line of sight.

I snickered at that and took a long drink with a satisfied smile. She could avoid looking at me all she wanted, that was fine with me.

"I can't believe she came back here," Lana said with a scoff.

"You're much more stunning than her," Tiffany said to me. "She's definitely jealous."

"Thank you," I said. "We'll just ignore her and enjoy ourselves, okay?"

They both nodded vigorously and held up their glasses so we could cheers.

The girls took turns telling me about themselves and I listened as well as I could while also paying attention to the game. An hour in and Jong-hyun was out.

He walked into the bar, up behind me, and slid his arms around my waist, resting his chin atop my head.

"Sorry you lost," I said and patted his forearm where it lay on my stomach.

"We all knew only one of us could win. I just had hoped to last longer."

"That's what she said," I snickered.

He chuckled and squeezed me. "Incorrigible."

"Want a drink?" I asked.

He nodded and released me.

"Let me move," Lana said and got up to sit on Tiffany's other side so Jong-hyun could sit on the stool beside me.

"Thank you," he said and took her vacated stool. The bartender came over and gave him a drink on the house for losing.

"I see *she* is here," Jong-hyun whispered as he raised his glass up to drink.

I shrugged a shoulder. "I assumed she would be."

He took a drink and watched me, brows furrowed.

"What?" I asked.

"You're much calmer than I expected you to be."

"Well, I can't go around causing scenes everywhere. I'll probably get arrested here if I bite someone's arm off."

He snickered and tweaked the end of my nose. "Most definitely."

"You bit someone's arm off?" Lana asked with a gasp.

I'd sort of forgotten they were there and listening. Whoops.

I turned and smiled. "They hurt my friend."

"Bad ass," Tiffany breathed out.

A group of men in suits walked into the bar, their movements smooth and languid, and their expressions full of confidence. They were definitely shifters, though I couldn't tell what kind. Walking together like that, they reminded me of the gangster movies Reed and I'd watched recently. They sat on the edge of the bar, a few seats away from Tiffany and Lana.

Jong-hyun gave them a once over and then resumed watching the match. If he wasn't worried about their presence then I would ignore them, too.

"We should get ice cream tonight, no matter what the outcome is," I suggested.

Jong-hyun nodded. "Okay," he answered me, but his focus was completely on the poker game.

The game moved so slow and I didn't fully understand it, so I spent more time chatting with Lana and Tiffany instead.

An explosion behind us shook everything and sent debris flying around.

Chaos immediately ensued as people, including Lana and Tiffany, started screaming and running in all directions.

Lana had been struck by debris and her leg bled profusely.

"Jong-hyun, carry her," I ordered him. "She's human."

Jong-hyun's eyes widened and while I could tell he wanted to stay by my side, he instead picked her up and carried her. Tiffany clutched his arm, staying at her friend's side as they started to make their way through the crowd and towards the exit.

I followed behind them, confident my other men would stay together and keep each other safe.

My concern should have been for myself as someone stabbed a knife into my lower left side.

I screamed and turned to see who it was, my shark skin beginning to cover my vital parts now that I realized I was in danger.

One of the suited men sneered at me. "Sorry, love, it's just business."

Movement in front of me made me turn and I thanked whatever gods might exist that my skin was so tough as another of the suited men tried to slash my chest with claws.

I'd never seen a paw like his before. He managed to tear my dress, which infuriated me, but my skin remained unmarred.

"Weak claws," I taunted and snapped my teeth at him, trying to put space between us, but the knife in my back slowed my movements.

He stabbed me in the stomach, his knife going right through to the same spot as the one in my back.

I screamed and fell to my knees as an odd fiery sensation spread from the place both knives touched inside my stomach.

"Kass!" Reed roared.

"Grab her," the first one who'd stabbed me ordered.

Two of suited men grabbed me and carried me in the opposite direction that everyone was running.

No. No, I would not be kidnapped. Never again.

Turning my head, I bit into the shoulder of the guy holding me, my teeth sinking straight to bone.

He screamed and made an odd cackling laughing sound and released me, dropping me to the ground.

"What the hell is she?" one of the others asked as I turned to try to bite him.

Grant and Reed grabbed the men and tossed them away from me, standing on either side of where I lay on the ground.

"Kass, how badly are you hurt?" Grant asked.

"Skewered," I panted on my knees. My vision started to get hazy with darkness encroaching on the edges. "It burns oddly. Poison, maybe."

"Who hired you?" Reed asked.

"Confidential," one of the men replied. He took out two

more knives from inside his suit jacket and smiled. "Please step aside. Our assassination has not been completed."

Grant and Reed growled and the deep bass sound vibrated through me.

Jong-min knelt beside me and said, "I'm going to have to pull them out, flower. It's going to hurt."

"It hurts to breathe with them inside me. Do it," I said.

The suited men tried to come forward, but Grant and Reed each shifted partially and fought against them.

I wanted to watch, to pay attention, but it was harder and harder to keep my eyes open.

Jong-min gripped both handles and jerked the knives from me simultaneously.

A scream tore out of my throat at the unbearable pain. The next second, I fell into Jong-min and the darkness consumed me.

18

I awoke with a start, jerking upright in the bed.

I lay on Grant's bed in the hotel room, but there was no one with me. Reaching down, I probed at my back and stomach, but there was no pain. Thank the stars for my fast healing.

"How can you even question who hired the assassins?" Grant snapped from the adjoining room. "There's no doubt it was the werewolves."

"We don't know that for certain," Reed replied, but I could hear the uncertainty in his tone.

"Who else would hire assassins to kill her? She doesn't have enemies here, except your pack," Grant said and growled.

I walked through the adjoining door, and four heads swiveled in my direction.

Jong-hyun rushed over and grabbed my hands in his. "I'm so sorry. I shouldn't have left you and –"

I leaned forward and kissed his lips. "Is Lana okay?"

He nodded. "She and Tiffany are safe."

"That's what's important. Thank you for getting them to safety."

"How are you feeling?" Grant asked as he walked to me and lifted my shirt to look at my stomach.

My skin was unblemished.

"I'm fine. Completely healed."

He exhaled loudly and pulled me into a tight hug. "I was so worried."

"Did you extract the poison from me?" I asked Jong-min who sat on the edge of his bed scowling.

He nodded once.

"Thank you."

"You don't need to thank me for that," he said.

I walked up to him and sat on his lap. "You used your magic to heal me, so yes, I will thank you."

He hugged me and kissed my cheek. "When you fainted, I was so worried you wouldn't wake up."

Smiling up at him, I said, "I'm not going anywhere, Tigerlily. You're stuck with me."

"Tigerlily?" he asked and his brows furrowed.

"We tried to get to you sooner, but the crowds were moving in all directions and it was hard to push against them," Reed said. He stood by the window, one hand pressed against it and his head hanging down.

"You protected me," I said. "That's all that matters." I walked up behind him and reached out to touch his shoulder, but he spun around and grabbed me in a crushing hug.

"I thought I'd lost you," he whispered into my hair. "Twice."

"Twice?" I asked as I hugged him back.

He nodded with his face buried against my neck. "When you started to break our bond and then when you fainted."

Oh, right.

"I'm safe and sound," I said. "Not even a scar."

He gripped me tighter and pressed his lips against the side of my neck. "I'm sorry, Kass."

I wasn't exactly sure what he was apologizing for, but I rubbed his back while he held me and said nothing.

His phone rang, ruining the moment as he stepped away to answer it. "Hello? Yeah, I'll be there soon."

"Where are you going?" Grant asked.

"The pack summoned me to give them my answer," he replied looking down at his phone.

"You're going to leave to meet with them now? After everything that happened?" Jong-min snapped. "Kass has assassins hired to kill her."

"The alpha has ordered me to come," Reed said softly.

Grant growled. "He stopped being your alpha when they banished you!"

Reed took a deep breath and walked out of the room without looking at any of us, leaving us standing together in stunned silence.

Needing to break the tension, I said, "I'm hungry. Healing takes a lot of energy out of me and requires a lot of calories to replenish that usage. Can we go eat somewhere?"

"We don't feel comfortable taking you out of the room while the assassins are still out there," Jong-min said. "We will order room service instead."

"Here." Jong-hyun held out the room service menu. "Order whatever you want."

Sitting on the edge of the bed, I looked over the menu. My stomach rumbled loudly, gaining their stares.

"Let's just order two of everything," Grant suggested and picked up the phone to call it in.

Jong-hyun sat on the bed beside me and picked up one of my hands from where they rested on my leg and linked it with his. "Are you certain you're healed?" The soft tone of his voice worried me. He was clearly still blaming himself for what had happened.

I squeezed his hand and smiled cheerfully at him. "I am certain."

He nodded and stared down at our joined hands.

"What happened with the final game?" I asked. "Did they postpone it?"

"Actually, we'd finished it right when the bomb went off," Jong-min said.

My eyes widened. "Who won?"

Grant raised his hand with a sheepish smile. "I did."

"Congratulations!" I shouted and jumped up to hug him.

He laughed and squeezed me back. "Thank you."

"That was a big pot to win, wasn't it? What are you going to do with it?"

"We've been discussing what to do with the money if any of us won since we got invited, actually," he admitted. "We were thinking of going on a trip to another country, but we weren't certain if you'd be able to handle the flight. I guess now we know you can."

"Flying is not fun, but I think I'll be able to handle it,

especially if it's to go on a fun vacation with you guys." I smiled broadly at them all, but they didn't really return the smile.

Were they thinking about whether the trip would include Reed still?

I knew I was.

Someone knocked on the door. Grant walked to it and looked through the peephole. "Room service sure is fast here," he said and opened the door.

The instant the door opened a smidge, the person on the other side kicked it all the way open and stormed inside. It was one of the suited men who'd tried to kill me.

Grant grabbed the guy by his jacket and started to throw him back out of the room, but four more men rushed inside.

Jong-min and Jong-hyun jumped to their feet, getting between me and the men. They moved so well together, in sync with each other with each punch, kick, and turn.

Now that I was prepared and not blindsided like yesterday, I stood and shifted into a half shift to give myself better defense from their blades and claws. My head shifted partially as well, my teeth lengthening to the length they'd be in my shark form, and I knew I looked really creepy with such a wide mouth and smile, but it was easier to bite this way.

Grant, Jong-min, and Jong-hyun fought against the men, but the fifth one, one of the ones who had stabbed me yesterday, got past them.

I smiled wide, showing off my teeth. "You won't catch me distracted this time, asshole."

His body shuddered and fur sprouted along his arms and

head as he took a half shift. His fur was brown with black spots and his head was a weird combination of feline and canine. He made that cackling, laughing sound and snarled at me. "You're going to die today, shark."

"What the heck are you?" I asked as I dodged his claws and punches.

"Hyena," he answered with the weird laugh again.

"The heck is a hyena?" I demanded and punched him in the stomach.

He let out an "oof" from my punch and drew a dagger. "Just let us kill you so we can earn our money."

"Pass," I said, spun behind him, and bit into his neck, killing him.

I let his body fall to the floor and turned to see that the others had defeated their opponents as well.

"Are you injured?" Jong-min asked.

"No, you?" I asked.

They all shook their heads.

"I'll call security," Jong-hyun said and walked to the nightstand where the phone was.

"Well, I guess we can go out to eat now," Grant said as he looked at the dead assassins. "They're not going to come after Kass again."

"Let me brush my teeth first," I said as I tried not to throw up. "Hyena tastes really weird."

19

Grant stayed back to talk to security and the cops, and to make sure the bodies were cleaned up before we returned.

I'd done a mouth wash after brushing my teeth to get the hyena taste out of my mouth. I wasn't sure what it was about his blood, but it tasted foul.

"You sure you aren't injured?" Jong-hyun asked for the fifth time.

We sat down at the table the maître d' escorted us to and I leaned over to kiss Jong-hyun's cheek. "The idiot tried to stab me with a knife, but didn't know my skin is super hard when I'm ready. The only reason I got skewered before was because they surprised me. How was I supposed to know that the explosion was a diversion so the assassins could come after me?"

"We'll have to start putting barriers up all the time," Jong-min said. He released a long and loud sigh. "You're so much trouble."

"You love me," I said with a wide smile.

His brows furrowed. "I never said I didn't."

"So, we fly out tomorrow, right?" I asked.

They both nodded.

"It'll be nice to be home." I was certain I was going to get an earful from Theo when she found out everything that had happened.

Silver was likely going to chastise me as well, but he'd give me a free drink while doing it.

Jong-min nodded. "Yes, it will be nice to be home. I miss my bed. This one is too hard."

I looked over at the grumpy male and asked, "Why didn't you say anything? You could have tried one of the others."

"It was not unbearable, plus that would have inconvenienced everyone." He shrugged. "I've slept on worse."

"I thought you were going to say slept *with* worse," I muttered.

He laughed softly, reached over, and linked his fingers with mine in my lap. "I'm a jerk, but not *that* much of a jerk."

"Debatable," I whispered and he squeezed my hand.

"Sorry that took so long," Grant apologized as he joined us. "Did you order yet?"

We shook our heads.

"Did they give you any trouble?" Jong-min asked.

Grant picked up the menu. "No, they have cameras that clearly showed we were attacked, and they have the video of the same men trying to assassinate Kass yesterday. Cut and dry case. They're moving us to a different room, though, because the cleaner group isn't available today."

"Good evening, can I get your drink order?" a petite

vampire with long, blonde hair asked. She wore a tuxedo and had adorable fangs that peeked out when she smiled.

"I wish I looked adorable like that," I whispered as I looked down at my menu.

Jong-min squeezed my hand and I flinched, realizing he had heard me.

The guys ordered their drinks and Jong-min ordered mine for me. I liked it when they ordered for me because oftentimes, I wasn't certain what I wanted and instead of contemplating for several minutes, they could order for me and if it was something I didn't want, I'd just order a new item.

"I'll be back to take your meal order once your drinks are ready," she said as she bowed at the waist, and floated away.

"You're far more adorable than her," Jong-hyun whispered as he leaned over, his warm breath blowing hair away from my ear.

"Thank you," I said and set my free hand onto his leg. He linked our hands together, so I now sat with my hand held by each of the twins. Twin heaven.

"Do you know what you want to eat?" Grant asked me.

"Everything, as long as it isn't hyena." My face scrunched up at the memory of the taste. "So gross."

"I've never had it, but I'll take your word for it," Jong-min said.

"I'll get you a few things, and we can take the leftovers back to the room for you to snack on," Grant said as he resumed looking back at the menu.

"You guys are the best." I let a contented sigh and relaxed back against my seat. I turned to Jong-min and said, "When we get back, I'd like to visit the restaurant and speak to my adopted parents."

He smiled. "I'm sure they will like that."

"I'm prepared to receive an earful from Mother," I said and smiled. "She will have so much to say to me about everything that's happened here."

"Theo will likely be the most vocal," Grant said.

I cringed. "Yeah, she's going to lecture me quite a bit. Honestly, I think one of the first things I want to do when we get back is talk to Zara and Zyra about training me." I'd done some training with them before, but they were … intense. Now, though, I was prepared and ready for it.

"Why them?" Jong-min asked. "Why not us?"

"The more varied people I train with, the better prepared I'll be for anything that comes at me. Clearly, my life isn't going to stay calm and collected like I'd wanted. It's become abundantly clear that I need to become stronger, better trained, and learn a few tricks to not only help me survive, but ensure all of you are protected."

"It's not your job to protect us," Jong-min countered.

"It is, too. As your mate, I need to protect you just like you want to protect me."

Three sets of eyes pinned me in place as I realized what I said.

"I mean, um, future mate," I corrected and looked down at the folded menu on the table.

"Call me that again when we're in the hotel room," Jong-min purred in my ear.

Grant shifted in his seat and leaned across the table with

eyes full of fire. "I'm tempted to bend you over this table right now."

I threw my head back as I laughed. "You guys are so bad."

"Your drinks," the waitress said and distributed them. "Are you ready to order?"

Grant nodded and placed an order for everyone.

It was the first time I'd seen him order for the twins, but neither seemed concerned or irritated. Had they started doing this without me noticing?

"Are we still going to do the jewelry making thing when we get back? I want to start learning about the hobbies you guys have and doing the hobby date things." We'd discussed it before coming here, but I still wanted to make sure.

Jong-min nodded. "I placed an online order for the supplies before we left. They are scheduled to arrive tomorrow."

I clapped my hands together and smiled wide. "Awesome! I can't wait to try to create some jewelry."

"Does it hurt to pull your teeth?" Jong hyun asked, a worried frown on his face.

"Not really," I said and shrugged. "If I really want to start a business of it, I'll go talk to the Chums and see if they'll give me teeth they lose, too." Cap'n Two-Teeth's Chums, were a ragtag pirate crew of shark shifters with a gambling and alcohol problem. Cap'n Two-Teeth was an old great white shark with one eye, a hook stuck in his dorsal fin, and only two teeth left in his decayed gums. Normally, he should have grown the teeth back, since great whites often shed teeth, but he'd pissed off the wrong selkie who had been owed a favor by a sea witch, and now was cursed to only have two teeth at any one given point. The crew were loyal to him without question and I loved them a ton. They'd gotten me through a lot when I was younger and I also needed to visit them more often, rekindle our friendship. Maybe I'd start going on swims with them again, like old times.

"Are you and Theo okay? I know you were upset about her choice of boyfriend." Jong-hyun looked at me curiously, a slight frown on his handsome face.

"Yes, we're okay. I voiced my concerns, so if she still wants to stay with him, then perhaps he really has changed." I *highly* doubted it.

"Hey guys," Reed said, and sat down beside Jong-hyun. "Sorry that took me so long."

We all stared at him expectantly, but he just smiled and waved down the waitress to place his order.

"Bro, spit it out. Are you going back to your pack or not?" Jong-min demanded once the waitress left.

He scowled and looked up at us. "Oh, um, well ..." He rubbed the back of his neck and smiled nervously. "I actually challenged the alpha to a fight and won, so technically, I'm alpha of the pack now."

"What!" I screeched.

20

"You're joking, right?" Jong-min demanded. "You wouldn't be so stupid."

"Hey, name calling is not okay," Reed growled.

"What were you thinking, Reed?" Grant asked. He put his face in his hands and shook his head. "If you wanted to fucking leave our pack, you could have just left. Why in all the stars would you want to become alpha of that fucked up group?"

"Everyone, take a breath," Jong-hyun instructed. "Let Reed speak."

Reed's brows were furrowed as he looked at all of us. "You guys should be praising me for my quick thinking. This was the only way to get out of the forced mating arrangement."

"As alpha, you're going to be expected to take a mate," I said, the words like rotten seal on my tongue.

Reed sighed and shook his head. "You guys clearly don't understand what the plan is."

"Enlighten us then," Jong-min snapped.

"Min," I whispered and squeezed his hand. "Let him talk."

He stroked his thumb across the back of my hand and remained silent.

Reed took a breath before beginning. "If I said I wasn't going to be her mate, she would be shamed as well, even though it has nothing to do with her. They take rejections like that very seriously and side with the males, making others think there's something wrong with the female even when there's extenuating circumstances. So, I challenged the alpha to a fight, won, and became the new alpha. As alpha, yes, I would be expected to take a mate, produce a litter of pups, and a ton of other duties. So, my first official decree once I became alpha was to pass on the title of alpha to the second in line and withdraw from the pack, becoming a rogue."

My eyes widened. Sharks didn't have packs or hierarchies like wolves and other land shifters did, but I knew that becoming a rogue was a huge deal.

"I was basically a rogue without the title as it was, so now that I have officially become a rogue, they can never come for me again. They can never try to force me into an arranged mating against my will again. It was the perfect solution. Now, I can be with my pack, my true pack, you three assholes." He smiled as he said it, letting his true feelings show.

Grant moved around the table and hugged him, patting him roughly on the back. "You had us worried, you jerk."

My fear wasn't abated, though. Sure, he'd declined being mated to her, but he hadn't said he'd done it for me or because of his love for me. Not that I had to be the reason, but where did that leave us?

As if sensing my concern, he looked over at me and his smile slowly slipped away. "I know I have a lot of ass kissing to do, a lot of apologies and presents to give you. It's true what they say, you don't realize what you have until it's gone. I'm glad that I realized it before you were completely gone. I'm sorry."

This wasn't really the best spot to have this discussion.

"I'm sorry I—"

"Let's finish talking later. I just wanted to explain what had happened since you guys assumed the worst," he said and smiled.

I returned his smile, but it felt a little forced as I still wasn't completely sure about ... everything.

The waitress came back and took Reed's order, and the guys started talking about plans for the poker money. I listened, but didn't really participate.

Jong-min kept our hands interlocked throughout the dinner, using his non-dominant hand to eat just to do so.

I appreciated it more than he knew.

When we went to our new rooms, Reed pulled me into his and shut the door, separating the others from us.

My pulse skyrocketed and I licked my lips.

He gently gripped my upper arms and pulled me into a warm, tight hug. "I'm so sorry, Kass. I'm a total asshole and I wish I had pulled my head out of my ass sooner. I caused you a lot of unnecessary pain that I'll always regret."

"I'm sorry I almost severed the bond. I wasn't really even sure what I was doing, it was just ... happening."

He leaned back and shook his head. "Don't apologize. I'm sure seeing me with her was painful, but I want you to know that absolutely none of my hesitation was due to being attracted to her or not being in love with you." He set his hand on the side of my face and smiled sweetly. "You're the greatest woman I've ever met and I wouldn't trade you for anything."

"We'll never be able to have pups," I whispered sadly.

He nodded. "I knew that when we started dating and my resolve to continue being with you hasn't changed. Can you forgive me?"

"Honestly, I want to say yes, but ... it hurts still." I looked down at his chest and he pulled me into a hug again.

"I'll earn back your trust, no matter how long it takes," he swore.

"Can we just ... cuddle and watch shows with everyone?" I needed the physical touch and group atmosphere.

"Anything you want, babe."

21

The flight back sucked a lot, but I survived and almost kissed the ground in relief after landing.

After dropping off the suitcases, we headed to Silver's to meet Theo. I'd promised her that I would see her as soon as I could and since the flight landed in the early evening, we'd agreed Silver's was the best place. Plus, I was in desperate need of a drink and a familiar, safe place to drink it in.

The bar was busy, but not unusually so, Tonka even welcomed me back and fist bumped my guys. We quickly found Theo seated at the bar talking to Silver with a big, burly man I didn't know beside her.

Silver spotted us first and whistled. "My daughter has returned from the land of sand!"

Several of the regulars cheered, which made me smile wide.

Theo hopped off her barstool. Her cute black skirt was paired with skull leggings, a bright pink sequin tank top, and a white wig. She'd also done her makeup flawlessly; the colors matched her outfit. "Kass!" she screamed as she rushed forward and hugged me.

I nearly fell due to her attempted tackle-hug, but managed to keep my balance. Laughter burst out of me and I squeezed her tight. "I don't think you missed me at all."

"You are going to make me go prematurely grey," she accused and stepped back, hands on her hips.

"Good thing you wear wigs all the time then," I said and winked.

Her cheeks puffed. "You had assassins after you! Assassins! Can't you just go on a calm, quiet vacation?"

"Apparently not," Jong-min muttered.

Reed walked up to the bar and smiled at Silver. "Evening, Silver. Can I get two old fashioneds and two of those new red beers?"

Silver looked at him and folded his arms over his chest. "I'm not sure you get a drink."

"Silver," I chastised as I walked over to stand beside Reed at the bar top. "Don't be hard on him."

"No, he's right. I have a lot of apologizing to do," Reed said and put an arm around my lower back. "I'll spend the rest of my life doing it, too."

Silver lowered his arms and nodded once before grabbing glasses to make the drinks Reed had ordered. "As long as you acknowledge your mistake and work towards rectifying it, that's good enough for me."

Turning to my left, I looked at the guy who'd been talking to Theo when we'd walked in. "Sorry, I didn't catch your name."

He smiled at me and a chill ran down my spine. "I'm Damien. It's nice to finally meet you, Kassidy."

As I shook his hand, realization hit me and I gasped, stumbling back away from him. "Or-Orca!"

"It's okay, he's not—" Theo tried to grab my shoulder, but I turned sideways before she could grab me. Fear coursed through me like lava in my veins and I stumbled away from her.

"What's wrong?" Jong-min asked as he and Jong-hyun came up behind me, standing protectively on either side of me.

Damien held up his hands placatingly. "I won't hurt you."

"The fuck kind of statement is that?" Grant demanded and snarled, turning around from the bar to glare at Damien. "Of course you won't hurt her. I'll tear your head off before you can hurt her."

"Everyone, calm down," Theo begged.

"What's going on?" Silver asked as he noticed our tense standoff. "Kass?"

Damien lowered his hand. "I understand why you're scared, but I don't have a pod and I don't mess with sharks. I know the others in this town are assholes so your experiences with orcas has been bad, but I'm not like them. I hate those cocky douche nozzles and how they continue to give us a bad name by being bullies and killers. Letting go of your prejudice may be hard, but you have to know that Theo wouldn't be dating me if I was like them, right?"

I wanted to believe that Theo would only date good people, but they hadn't known each other that long, so he could be hiding his crazy. However, his words felt sincere and I had never seen him with the pod here.

My shoulders slumped a bit as I relaxed. "I'm sorry, I shouldn't have reacted that way."

He smiled. "It's understandable when you've dealt with the pod here. They're psychopaths who bully me as well."

"We should team up and kick their asses," I said returning his smile. "I've got a dragon who could pluck them out of the sea and dangle them up in the sky."

He laughed and everyone else in the group relaxed fully. "That would be fun to witness."

Holding out my hand, I said, "It's nice to meet you, Damien."

As he shook my hand, Theo wrapped her arms around my shoulders and rested her head against mine. "I'm sorry. I should have warned you."

Dropping Damien's hand, I turned to face her and shook my head. "No, I've got to stop being so prejudiced against others. I have to stop letting fear run my life."

"You haven't had the best track record with a lot of the sea life here," she said. "Sometimes I consider just cursing each and every one of them."

Laughing, I shook my head. "You'd run out of magic before you made it through that list."

She joined my laughter and I hugged her again. I wasn't one hundred percent convinced that Damien was clean, but Theo was a big girl who could handle herself. Plus, I had to really stop allowing fear to win so often with me.

"Get your drink," Silver ordered me, "and update me on everything that happened on your trip."

22

"I've got some good news and bad news," Stacy said as I climbed out of the tank at the end of my shift. She held out a towel for me to dry off and looked down at the ground sheepishly.

In all the years that we'd worked together, she'd never looked down when I came out, even though I was always naked. Something about her behavior had my nerves on edge.

"What's up?" I asked and quickly got dressed just in case she'd suddenly developed a case of shyness. I didn't want someone I considered a friend to feel uneasy around me. Just because something had been okay before didn't mean it was now.

"I'm leaving the aquarium," she blurted.

My head had just popped through the hole in my shirt at her announcement and my mouth immediately dropped open. "What? Where are you going? When? Why? Is it me?"

She held up her hands to stop my barrage of questions. "I found my mates, but they live across the country," she explained quickly, her cheeks turning bright pink as she fiddled with the bottom of her shirt. "I'm moving in with them."

I threw my arms around her shoulders and hugged her tightly. "Congratulations! That is so exciting!"

"You don't hate me?" she asked as she looked up and met my eyes.

She'd obviously been worrying about breaking the news to me, but only a jerk would be upset at someone for following their heart.

"How could I be mad that you found your mates? That's the best news anyone could receive."

"Well, there is one more thing," she said and stepped back. "My replacement is here and she wants to meet you."

Her replacement...

It made sense that they would have to replace her, but now *I* was the one worried. What was she like? Would she like me? Would she be as nice and understanding as her? Thank goodness I just took that vacation with the guys or this new person might have denied it and ruined my chances of getting Reed to stay.

"Okay, let me dry my hair a bit more and we can go meet her." As quickly as I could, I wrung out my hair, towel dried it, and put it up into a ponytail. Once I was certain that I was presentable, I followed her to her office.

My heart rate picked up as we approached, nerves I hadn't felt in a long time.

Reed and Grant watched me walk by with their brows furrowed as if they could sense my tension. Perhaps they could. Our connection was a bit of an odd one. Our emotions sometimes filtering through, but not all the time.

The office was small, just meant for her to work on her computer as she didn't handle the high-level clients here, that was done by the higher ups, and she preferred to take her tablet with her as she walked around the aquarium to keep it in working order.

Inside of the office stood a woman with her back to us, a turquoise green dress wrapped tightly around her body, flaring out into a mermaid style with pearls on the hem. Her hair was a vibrant turquoise similar to the dress that reminded me of someone, but I couldn't place who.

"I've brought Kass, our star, our tiger shark, to meet you, just as you've asked," Stacy said brightly.

The woman spun around, her hair flaring out around her as she did. My heart sank as I spotted the one arm which was missing after the elbow.

Koia. The mermaid who was Theo's worst enemy and the one I'd bitten an arm off of.

Shit.

She smiled sweetly. "Thank you, Stacy. Can you give us a moment alone?"

Stacy looked from my shocked face to Koia and frowned. "Alone? You want me to leave? I assure you that whatever you have to say, you can say in front of me."

Koia's smile turned into a baring of teeth. "Fine. Kass, it's clear you've made a big impact on the aquarium, your exhibit was one of the most visited last year. However, recently the visits to your exhibit have dwindled, the jellyfish have become more of a draw."

"I was on vacation, so the children thought I was sick. Now that they know I'm back, I'm certain this month's visits will increase." I raised my chin, refusing to give in. My children visitors loved me and came back often to see me as well as to buy merchandise. With the addition of the live feed camera, our merchandising had doubled thanks to online orders.

"You know what sells even better?" she asked as she took a step forward, her eyes dark with malice.

"What?" I asked when it was clear she wouldn't continue without prompting.

"Death. Memorialization."

"What?" Stacy gasped.

"Excuse me?" My teeth lengthened at the threat and I prepared to defend myself if necessary. I liked my job, but I would destroy her before she could hurt me.

Koia spun, her hair flicking me in the face as she did, and walked over to the desk. "Yes, the design team spent all day coming up with these new items, which I'm certain we will sell out of quickly. Your death will be mourned by all and your memory will live on forever, as merchandise."

"What are you talking about?" Stacy asked.

Koia picked up a board with images of new products, ones that were for Kass, the tiger shark, with the years I'd supposedly been alive and my death listed as this year.

"You're going to kill me off so you can fire me," I realized, "while still making money off of my image."

Koia clapped her hands together and smiled wide. "Exactly!"

"Kass still gets royalties on those sales, even if you fire her from being an exhibit in the tank," Stacy said sternly.

Koia nodded. "Of course. Of course. We'd never think about not giving you what you're owed. In fact, we're going to give you a nice severance package as well in addition to a five percent raise on your merchandise royalty rate. It's our way of thanking you for helping the aquarium become what it is today."

I should have bitten off her head instead of her arm.

23

"I'm going to curse her so that no male or female will ever want to touch the disgusting fish and she will die sad and alone!" Theo shouted and slammed her glass down on the bar.

Silver turned from where he was serving a patron at the other end of the bar with a scowl.

Theo held up her hands and mouthed, "Sorry."

"I'm telling you, Theo, I think I'm cursed. How could Koia of all people come to be the manager of the aquarium I worked at?"

I tossed back the rest of my drink and slid it close to the edge, so Silver could grab it easily to refill it. I sniffled and wiped at my eyes. I'd sworn I wouldn't cry about this, but I loved that job, and losing it hurt a lot more than I wanted to admit to anyone, even Theo.

Theo hugged me and patted my back. "I'm so sorry, Kass. What did the guys say?"

I flinched as I remembered their anger. It had taken me five minutes to convince them not to quit their jobs at the aquarium as well. We couldn't afford for three of us to lose our income. "Not well. They wanted to quit, but I convinced them not to." With a big sigh, I laid my head on my arms and said, "It'll just be me trying to find a new job."

My prospects were pretty low. I couldn't put that I'd been an exhibit at the aquarium on a resume, and not having a job for so many years would raise a lot of red flags to potential employers.

"You could work here," Silver offered.

I raised my eyes and smiled. "I appreciate it, old man, but this is my place of relaxation. If I worked here, I'd no longer be able to relax here."

He nodded. "I can understand that."

"What about your mom and pop's? I know the twins have been working for them, but I'm sure you could be of assistance as well," Theo suggested.

She wasn't wrong, but ...

"I don't like taking money from them."

Silver and Theo sighed and shook their heads.

I sat up and glared at them. "Wow, double doses of disappointment. Rude."

Silver set down my new drink and asked, "What do you plan to do if not work for them?"

"She's going to work for me," Gina said as she sat on the barstool next to me.

We all turned to look at the sea witch.

"What?" I asked.

She smiled. "I need good help and you know how to

handle the jerks in this town. Really, you'd be doing me a favor by coming and working for me."

"I don't know the first thing about working in a pizza shop." Not that I didn't want the job, but I also didn't just want charity or to cause her issues.

"It's easy. Come by tomorrow and I'll give you the run down. We can do a week trial and you can let me know if you want to continue or not at that point. What do you say?"

It was the best option I had at the moment, plus, it would mean free pizza. Who didn't love free pizza?

"Are you sure?" I asked. "I don't want you to do this just because you feel bad or something."

She smirked. "Kass, dear, haven't you heard the expression to never look a gift horse in the mouth? Just come by tomorrow at ten o'clock, okay?"

"Silver, put her drinks on my tab," I said quickly and hugged her. "Thank you."

Gina smiled wide and clinked her glass against mine. "Can I join you in drinking the night away to mourn the loss of your job?"

"I wouldn't have it any other way," I said, smiling wide.

Two hours later, once Reed and Grant had gotten off of work, they joined us at Silver's bar.

"How long have you been drinking?" Reed asked me, stepping up behind me so that my ungraceful flail didn't cause me to fall off my barstool and just caused me to fall against his warm, firm, delicious chest.

Spinning on the barstool, I looked up at the frowning male and said, "I started when I got fired by that bitch."

"You need food," he commented and held up a bag of delicious smelling takeout. "I've got your favorite chicken noodles in here."

"You know the rules," Silver said. "No food in here."

"I know, I just needed the smell to entice her to go outside to eat it," Reed explained.

Silver snorted. "Smart man."

Grant draped an arm around my shoulders and kissed the side of my head as we left the bar.

Following Reed, eyes focused on the bag of food he was swinging as he walked, we headed out of the bar and down the street to the park, so I could sit at a table to eat.

I sat and quickly opened the takeout container, drooling at the scent, and quickly opened the plastic wrapper around the spork.

Reed sat across from me and Grant sat beside me, both frowning and looking worried.

"How are you doing?" Reed asked, watching as I shoveled a huge bite of chicken and noodles into my mouth.

I shrugged. "I'm annoyed, but Gina offered me a job, pending a one week trial period."

His eyes widened. "Wow, that was fast."

Chuckling, I nodded. "I was pretty surprised by the offer. Honestly, I'm just glad I won't be losing much income."

"I'm more worried about your mental status than money," Grant said.

Sighing, I set my fork down and looked at them fully. "I'm pretty bummed, I liked my job, and I'm going to miss the kids. I'm also upset that the kids will be upset thinking I'm dead, but there's not much I can do. I shouldn't have been working there to begin with, they could get in a lot of trouble if they admitted that they'd hired a shifter to act as an aquarium exhibit. I had it pretty easy up until now, and I'm worried I won't be able to handle a real job."

"You underestimate yourself, babe. You're going to do great, and it won't be harder than when you help your parents at their restaurant," Reed said and squeezed my hand.

"Speaking of your parents," Grant said. "You still going to visit them tomorrow?"

I nodded. "Yep, which works pretty well since Gina's is right by their place."

Reed's phone beeped and he opened it to read the message he'd received. "The twins are headed to the bar."

"I better eat fast, then!" Picking the spork back up, I ate my food quickly, but not quick enough to make myself sick or give myself indigestion.

I didn't finish it all, but Grant quickly tipped the container up and ate the rest of it with ease.

After throwing the trash away in the cans, we headed back to the bar to meet the twins.

We ran into them outside, arguing with a man who looked similar to the twins, though a bit older.

"Hey!" I greeted as I skipped up to them.

The man turned and glared at me.

"We'll meet you inside in a minute," Jong-min told me.

"Okay," I said and turned to head inside, high-fiving Tonka, the half-troll half-orc bouncer who had become a friend after I'd saved the city from Bastian.

"Is this whore the reason you've been ignoring our letters?" the man asked loudly.

24

I paused, foot up in mid-skip, and turned to look at the man.

Grant and Reed growled.

Jong-min growled and said, "Apologize right now! You can be angry at us, but you do not disrespect Kassidy."

The man continued to glare at me, but said, "Sorry."

"I'm sorry. We'll be in after we talk to him," Jong-hyun said and kissed my cheek. "Family drama," he whispered before he pulled back and smiled at me.

Grant intertwined our fingers on one hand and pulled me into the bar. "That's their brother."

That explained the similarity in appearance.

"All fed and happy?" Silver asked.

"Yes," I said with a nod, determined not to let anything get me down again tonight. "Where's Theo?" I asked, looking around.

"She and Gina went into the pool room," he said before heading over to a new patron, who walked up on the opposite end of the bar.

Theo and Gina walked out of the pool room, cash in Theo's hand. I gasped and said, "You cheated on me?"

She put the money behind her back, eyes wide. "Uh, no?"

Fake sniffling, I asked, "How could you? I thought what we had was special?"

"Look, sometimes your partner just needs a change, okay? Or is the reason you're upset because you're worried she'll like me better?" Gina sashayed by me and leaned against the bar top with a smirk.

"So cruel," Grant said and shook his head. "You poor, poor thing."

"I swear, it was just this once," Theo said, continuing our joke.

"Liar. You've probably cheated on me with others when I wasn't here to catch you in the act," I fake sobbed.

"A girl's got to eat," Theo said with a shrug.

Immediately, we all burst into laughter.

"Another round," Theo called out to Silver and set a one hundred on the counter.

Jong-min and Jong-hyun walked in, heads together, whispering, and scowling.

Jong-min pushed Grant out from behind me and wrapped his arms around my waist, to hug me from behind. "I'm sorry about my brother. He's upset with us because we cut off most of our communication with them."

I patted his arm that was around my stomach. "It's okay. It's not the first and definitely won't be the last time I've been called a whore. Did you guys work out your issues?"

"We're going to meet him tomorrow after work to talk more," Jong-hyun answered and kissed me on the temple.

"Speaking of tomorrow, I'll be coming by the restaurant in the afternoon," I advised them.

"Oh?" Jong-min asked.

"After she comes to work for me," Gina added from beside us.

"Work for you?" Jong-hyun asked, looking back and forth between us.

"Gina offered me a job," I explained.

"Do you need a job if you're going to get royalties?" Jong-hyun asked.

I nodded. "The royalties won't be enough to sustain me, plus I can't be certain how much I'll get each month. I'd rather not be worried about it every month and just use that as savings or bonus cash when I do get the royalty payments."

"That's smart," Theo said.

"I have smart ideas occasionally," I replied and flipped my hair over my shoulder, accidentally smacking Jong-min in the face with it, which made us all laugh.

I arrived at Gina's place at nine o'clock like she asked. Thankfully, I wasn't super hungover even though I had drunk a lot the night before to drink away my blues.

"Morning!" Gina called out as she walked into the walk-in fridge when I entered through the backdoor.

"Morning," I replied.

She exited the fridge, three of her tentacles sticking out

from under her dress, each carrying a bucket. "So, I didn't really talk to you about it last night, but I don't want you to work here and cook. I want you to work here as a manager."

"A manager?" I asked, eyes wide.

She nodded. "I have enough workers who can make the pizzas and they get paid starting wages. What I need you for is to manage them and manage the customers. Basically, my other employees will run the back of the shop here, while you run the front of the shop. So, let me give you a rundown on things. Then, we can talk money and I'll have you sign some paperwork. Okay?"

I nodded. "Yes, ma'am."

It only took her ten minutes to explain things to me, but the register was the hardest part for me to learn because she was stubborn and hadn't gotten a new one in a decade. Once I finally did learn it, we went to her office so I could fill out the paperwork. She offered me more than I anticipated, so I gladly and gratefully accepted.

After that was finished, we exited the office and she introduced me to the first shift workers, Tyler and Marie.

"Kass is our new manager, so be nice to her and cut her some slack as she learns the ropes," Gina said and patted my shoulder.

"Be extra mean and expect her to know everything now, got it," Marie said with a smile.

"Marie likes to joke to try to make the day go by smoother," Tyler said and sighed. "It makes it go by slower."

Marie rolled her eyes. "Only because you don't appreciate my humor."

"Kass will be starting her first day tomorrow," Gina informed them. "Nine o'clock sharp tomorrow, okay?"

I nodded. "You got it, boss." Waving, I headed out and down the street to my parents' restaurant.

As soon as I opened the door, Mom started yelling at me, but it was in her native language, which I did not understand.

"Hello, Mother. It's nice to see you, too!" I said with a wide smile as I walked up and hugged her.

She sighed and hugged me back. "You've been away too long."

"Are my handsome boyfriends not helping enough? Do I need to beat them?"

She rolled her eyes. "Dramatic as always. We all know you don't beat them."

"How are you?" I asked and leaned against the counter. "And where's Dad?"

"He's in the back. I'm fine. When are you getting mated?"

Snorting, I shook my head. "When I'm asked, I suppose."

Her eyes widened. "Do they know you feel that way?"

I shrugged. "Most likely."

"Hm, I do not think so. I will find out."

"You can't just ask them, Mom."

"Course I can," she said and patted my arm. "I find out for you."

Shaking my head, I changed the subject. "How's the restaurant? Getting enough business?"

"Oh, yes. Lots of business with the twins here. Lots of female customers." She smiled when she noticed my irritation. "If you mated them, you wouldn't have to worry about the female customers."

"I got a new job," I told her to change the subject. "I'm working at Gina's now."

"Twins told us," she said and smirked. "They give me updates knowing you won't. That means you come by more, yes?"

"Yes," I said and nodded.

"Good."

"Hello," Dad said as he walked out of the back, wiping his hands on a towel. "How are you?"

"I'm good," I replied and walked over to hug him. "How are you?"

"Old," he said and sighed. "Good thing the twins help."

"Yes, I'm glad they've been helping you." It really did take a huge weight off my shoulders to know they were here.

"Speaking of that, we have news," Dad said. He glanced at Mom. "You tell her yet?"

Mom shook her head. "I was going to wait until you got here."

My stomach tightened nervously. "What's going on?"

"We are going home," Dad said when it became clear Mom didn't want to tell me.

"Home?" I frowned. "Are you not feeling well? Do you need me to run the shop tonight?"

"No, not our house here. Our homeland," Mom explained. "My sister is ill and we are going to return to be with her."

"How long will you be gone?" Since I was just starting

with Gina, I could help the twins run the restaurant while they were gone without issue.

"We aren't returning, Kassidy," Dad said softly. "The journey is difficult and so we have decided to stay there."

25

I blinked as I absorbed what my parents had said. "So, you're going to return to your homeland and not return? When are you leaving?"

"In a week or so," Mom said. "We're finalizing the flight details still."

My mouth dropped. "Why were you worried about me visiting if you're leaving so soon?"

"We'd like to see you as much as we can before we leave," she answered. Out of the side of her mouth she mumbled, "It'd be nice to see you mated before we left, too."

"Ay, you can't rush her," Dad said and tsked.

"When did you guys decide on this?" I asked.

"Just a few days ago," Dad answered. "We've been thinking about returning for a long time, but when we heard she was sick, we knew it was time. Plus ..." He smiled. "... you're all grown and even if you aren't mated, you have a good support system here even if we do leave."

"The bartender is gruff, but he good to you and can help you more than we can," Mom said with a nod.

Taking a deep breath, I absorbed the news and asked, "What do you need me to do to help you prepare to leave? Are you selling the restaurant?"

"Well, that's the other news," Dad said and glanced at Mom who nodded. "We're selling to the twins."

My mouth dropped. "What?"

They both nodded.

"They confirmed yesterday and signed papers," Mom answered.

The back door opened as the twins walked in.

"Speak of the devils," I said and put my hands on my hips.

They both looked at me in shock.

"Oh, uh, you told her?" Jong-hyun asked softly.

"Why didn't you tell me you were doing something so important?" I asked. What other crazy life decisions had they made without telling me? We weren't mated yet, but we were dating so I'd thought they would tell me things like this.

"We decided to use part of our share of the winnings from the poker tournament to buy the restaurant," Jong-min explained. "We were talking amongst ourselves, before you got fired actually, about wanting a business that was ours. One our pack could run so we didn't have to worry about finding jobs. When you got fired because of that slimy mermaid, we knew it was the right decision."

"We didn't tell you yet because your parents wanted to tell you about their trip first," Jong-hyun added as he walked closer and took my hands.

"Does this mean I won't be working for Gina?" I asked.

They both shook their heads. "Actually, we think it would be good for you to work elsewhere. We know you get worried about money so having a separate stream of income will give you ease of mind," Jong-min explained.

He was right, damn him.

"So, you four will work here?" I asked.

They both nodded.

Jong-hyun squeezed my hands. "And if you decided you want to come work here, you can. We just want you to have options."

"Is that why your brother is here?" I asked.

"Your brother here?" Mom gasped.

"He'll leave soon," Jong-min said with a scowl. "He came unannounced to try to convince us to return to our homeland."

"You don't want to go?" Dad asked.

Jong-min shook his head and Jong-hyun put his arm around me, hugging me against his side.

"We were not happy there and going back now will not change that," Jong-min answered. He looked at me and his lip twitched in a smile. "Plus, we have something here we won't give up."

"So, you do want to mate!" Mom shouted.

I facepalmed and groaned, "Mom."

"We need to talk about a few things with your parents about the restaurant and things. We're going to have a pack discussion tonight. Can you go to the store and pick up steaks and vegetables for dinner?" Jong-min asked me.

They were clearly trying to get rid of me, but it was okay because I needed to get some items from the store anyway.

"Sure," I said with a nod, and kissed all four on the cheek. "I'll come by tomorrow," I promised my parents.

They nodded and followed the twins towards the office in the side of the restaurant.

A pack owned restaurant would mean they wanted to stay here for an extended period of time. Did that mean they were ready to commit to being mated?

I hadn't talked to them about it recently, but I was more than ready to accept them as my mates, too.

Inside the grocery store, I waved to the employees I knew, grabbed a cart, and started my shopping. If this was a serious pack discussion, like it sounded like it was, I wanted to get something really delicious for dinner. Steaks were good, but I wanted lobster, too, as well as something yummy for dessert.

Staring at the bakery displays, I tapped my lips as I debated what to get.

"Don't accept," a male, accented voice said behind me.

I turned and smiled at the twins' brother. "Hello, brother of my boyfriends."

He hissed. "It is ridiculous they are dating you."

"You don't even know me," I said and put a hand on my hip. "Besides, it's not up to you what they do. They're adults and capable of making their own decisions."

"Why won't you just let them go?" he asked with a scowl.

"Uh, because I love them, duh." I scoffed and rolled my eyes. "If you don't have anything nice to say, then you can leave me alone."

"Don't accept their offer to be mated," he said urgently. "Please."

One of the bakery workers came out, wiping her hands on a cloth. "Are you ready?"

"Can you give me that chocolate cake?" I requested and pointed at the one in the display case with bright flowers decorated on it.

"Certainly," she said and grabbed a box to put the cake in.

"You aren't good enough for them and they're going to ask you to be their mate! It's insane!" he snapped behind me.

Sighing, I turned and said, "What's insane is you thinking you can come here and tell me what to do. What's insane is you going behind your brothers' backs to try to ruin the happiness they've found." Smiling to show my shark teeth I said, "We've fought for this happiness and I'm not going to let you or anyone else ruin it. If you want to talk to someone, go talk to your brothers."

He took a step closer, his body starting to glow as he drew on his magic. Cat ears popped up from his head and his hands turned into lion paws with large claws. "You will listen to me."

With a deep sigh, I pulled out my phone, videocalled Jong-min, and turned the camera to face his brother. "I have a situation," I said.

Jong-min growled loud and started shouting in their native language.

His brother reverted to human form, saying something softly back.

I turned the camera towards myself and made a kissy face at him. "See you at home."

"Smack him upside the head if he says anything else," he ordered me.

I saluted him. "Yes, sir!"

He muttered something in his language I'd heard quite a few times and was pretty sure was akin to, "crazy woman."

Taking the boxed cake from the worker, I smiled and said, "Have a wonderful day."

Cake obtained, I skipped to the checkout line. I was determined not to let anyone ruin my day. Especially not a grumpy feline shifter who didn't know me.

Especially when it seemed like our pack discussion tonight might involve a mating discussion. No, it would, because even if they didn't bring it up. I one hundred and thirty percent would.

26

By the time all of the guys finished work, came home, and changed clothes, I had dinner ready and on the table.

I'd also put just a little bit of makeup on and changed into my favorite jeans and a comfortable black t-shirt I had stolen from Grant. I had first stolen it because it smelled like him, but now I wore it because it was something of his. I had a shirt from each of the guys in my room now that they had seemed to accept were now mine. Reed had also given me his largest sized sweater that I wore when we hung out on the couch watching shows and relaxing.

"This smells delicious," Reed said and kissed me on the side of my head as he one-arm hugged me.

"Hopefully it tastes as good as it smells," I said as we all took seats at the dining table.

Jong-min and Jong-hyun suddenly stood and went to the door.

Reed, Grant, and I looked at each other curiously. Since

they looked at confused as me, that meant they hadn't expected a visitor either.

The twins returned with their brother behind them. He bowed his head and said, "I apologize for my rude behavior up to this point."

He was here to ruin my plans to talk about becoming mates!

"We invited him for dinner because he is here alone and because of some other things we'll discuss shortly," Jong-min explained.

"What's your name?" I asked.

The three looked at each other, realizing they hadn't officially introduced him to us yet.

"I am Jong-kyu," he said and tried to smile, but it was so forced I almost laughed.

"It's nice to officially meet you, Jong-kyu. I'm Kassidy."

"You know us," Reed grunted, arms folded across his chest, clearly not happy with Jong-kyu being here.

Jong-hyun grabbed a chair and set it at the table, grabbing a plate as well.

"Let's eat before it gets cold. Kass put a lot of work into this," Jong-min said. He grabbed my plate and filled it up, set it back in front of me, and then filled up his own plate.

Jong-kyu watched it happen with his eyes narrowed, but instead of commenting, filled up his plate as well.

I had planned to take less food since there was an additional person that I hadn't accounted for, but Jong-min had prevented that. Instead, the three brothers split up their food between them.

We ate in silence, but it was happy silence for me as I could tell everyone genuinely liked the food.

As soon as everyone was done, Grant and Reed stood, stacked all the dirty dishes, and took them to the sink.

"I got dessert," I announced.

"Cake?" Jong-hyun asked hopefully.

"Chocolate," I said with a nod.

His eyes sparkled and he quickly went to the cupboard for plates.

"Dinner was really good. Your cooking has definitely improved," Jong-min praised and slipped an arm around my waist.

Tilting my head back to look up at him, I smiled and raised on tiptoe to kiss his cheek. "Thank you." Leaning into his hold, I relished the rare moment of affection and praise from the notoriously grumpy male.

"Let's take the cake to the living room so we can talk," Jong-min said.

Grant and Reed helped carry the plates while Jong-min steered me out of the kitchen and to the living room.

"You've helped enough for today, darling," he whispered in my ear.

"I can just sit and look pretty now?" I teased.

He kissed the tip of my nose. "Yes."

The high level of sweetness worried me a bit. Was he buttering me up for bad news?

He sat down on the couch first and instead of sitting next to him, I sat on his lap, turned sideways with my legs draped over the arm of the couch. I rested the side of my head against his shoulder, my nose near his throat to draw in his scent better.

At first he tensed, but once I was comfortable and still, he wrapped his arms around me and stroked his fingers along the skin he had access to, which was mainly my forearm and leg.

Jong-kyu, who had followed us into the room, didn't like it judging by his thinned lips, but he smartly kept quiet and sat on the couch opposite us.

The others joined us and while I knew this was an important meeting, I let my eyes close and relished the moment with Jong-min as he explained to the others about my parents leaving and the restaurant now being theirs ... ours.

"So, we can quit the aquarium?" Reed asked.

"Yes," Jong-min answered with a nod.

"Finally," Reed exhaled.

"This is great news!" Grant exclaimed. "We finally have a pack business like we always wanted."

"We'll have to come up with a restaurant name," Jong-min said, "but that can come later."

My eyes opened as I started coming up with names to share.

"You know, if you advertised that you two, former pop star idols, are running the restaurant, you'd get a lot of customers coming. Your former fans would come in droves for a chance to be served food by you," Jong-kyu said, a smirk on his face.

He was clearly trying to make me jealous or mad. He obviously didn't know me.

Sitting up, I said, "That's a great idea! You could even help out with the tourism in this area by drawing in more visitors from your homeland."

Jong-kyu scowled, his plan thwarted by my acceptance.

"Oh!" I gasped and looked at Jong-min, who was smiling at me. "Do you have any of the outfits you two wore while on stage? You could wear one of them during the grand opening to *really* draw in customers! Even do photo ops! There're so many ways you could use your former fame to help the restaurant really take off. I mean, having four hot males like you there will be enough of a draw, but wearing suits or tuxedos or things like that would increase it even more."

"Being unmated would be the ultimate draw for their fans," Jong-kyu said and folded his arms over his chest.

"Speaking of that!" I said, stood, and went to the side table where I had stashed the presents. Walking to each of my four men, I set a present in each of their laps.

"What is this?" Grant asked, bending forward to look at the small wrapped gifts.

"I, Kassidy of Atlantis, tiger shark, pool shark, and outcast, officially ask for Grant, Reed, Jong-min, and Jong-hyun to accept me as mates. In your laps are your mating gifts, if you accept."

Despite my flawless delivery, wide smile, and straight back, it was all false confidence. There was still a huge part of me that worried they would decline.

All four of their eyes widened.

Jong-kyu's mouth had dropped open in disbelief. He said, "This is not how it is done! They are supposed to ask you."

I scoffed. "This isn't the old days."

My nerves grew as all four looked at each other and at the presents on their laps, but still didn't respond. Standing there, I felt my heart start to sink. Were they really not going to accept? After everything we'd been through?

Jong-min stood, set his gift on the coffee table next to his slice of cake, and walked out of the room.

Despair coursed through me, my heart felt like it had fallen through my stomach and through the floor of the house. I rarely cried, but tears threatened as my eyes burned.

After everything we'd been through, they still weren't ready? Even after the poker tournament and all the things that had tested us there and shown we're better together? They all swore they loved me, that I was the only female they had eyes for. So why were they hesitating?

What was it about me that they still had doubts? Was it my job? Was it because of my infertility? Why?

Why was I still not good enough?

I took a step back, ready to flee, but Jong-min returned with a small box in his hand with a teal bow atop it.

Stopping in front of me, he held out the box on an upturned palm. "We were going to give this to you later, but now seems better."

As I reached for it, my hand shook. Jong-min noticed, scowled, and gently grabbed my hand with his free hand. Squeezing, he whispered, "Open the box, Kass."

Box in my hand, I untied the teal bow and opened the box. My eyes widened and I gasped as I stared at the ring inside.

"We accept your mating offer and offer you this ring as our mating gift," Jong-min said softly.

Tears fell as the whirlwind of emotions over the last minute hit its crescendo. "When you left the room I ..."

He put the ring on my finger, pulled me into a hug, and whispered in my ear, "I love you, Kassidy tiger shark. And while it may have taken us longer than it should have, we don't want to be without you ever again. I know I was the most resistant at first, but at the end of the day the one thing I look forward to the most is coming home to you."

Jong-hyun hugged me from behind and kissed the back of my head.

Grant and Reed came forward as well and pried the twins off me to hug me next.

"We're sorry we froze, but you'd ruined our plan," Grant whispered in my ear.

"We'd planned to surprise you later with the ring and ask you to be our mate," Reed said and rubbed his cheek against mine. "You seem to always surprise us when we least expect it."

Chuckling, I wiped my tears on his shoulder. "Sorry."

"Really? You're taking her as a mate? All four of you are sharing one woman. A shark shifter on top of that? Not even a land shifter like you all?" Jong-kyu demanded.

"Love doesn't care what race they are. Love can see past all inconsequential things to show you the true value of a partner," Jong-hyun said. "Kass is smart, brave, kind, and would destroy the world for us."

I nodded emphatically. "Torch it to the ground."

"And we would do the same for her," Jong-min said. He reached forward and gripped my hand. "We almost lost her twice and it opened our eyes to a world without Kass. A world that would be devoid of meaning."

Squeezing his hand, I sniffled and said, "You're going to make me cry again."

"Let's sit and finish our discussion, yeah?" Jong-min said with a smile at me.

Nodding my agreement, I planned to sit between the twins, but Reed pulled me to the couch he and Grant sat on and tucked me between them, nuzzling my cheek and kissing it.

Jong-hyun brought out a notepad as they discussed what types of food they wanted to serve, restaurant theme, and other items, marking it all down in the notepad.

"The reason we brought Jong-kyu here tonight was because he has decided to live here for a while and he is going to work at the restaurant as well," Jong-min explained. "Any objections?"

"Nope," I said and Grant and Reed shook their heads.

During the discussion, Grant opened the gift I'd given him and immediately put the magical ring on. It would change size and shape when they shifted, to ensure they didn't cut off a finger or something when they shifted. They weren't cheap, but I'd been saving up for them for a while, plus the severance pay from the aquarium had helped me refill my savings so it didn't hurt as much.

When the others noticed the gift was also a ring, they all, while still talking, opened their boxes and put their rings on.

Looking around the room at my four soon to be mates, all

wearing the rings I'd gifted them, I couldn't stop smiling wide and I wasn't sure I ever would.

We still had to go through the official mating process, but as all our rings glistened on our fingers, it was the best sight of my life. A sight I had never thought possible.

27

With my parents leaving so soon, the guys went into hyper mode to finalize their plans, including the menu, purchase items, create advertisements, and preparing for the grand re-opening.

All of that meant that our official mating was put on hold until we had time and weren't rushed. None of us wanted to rush the mating, and it was enough for us to have our rings and have officially accepted each other.

As tourist season opened, a flood of annual visitors and new ones came to the city. Gina's was so busy that we had a line out the door each day. There was no time for me to think or do more than focus on taking orders, serving drinks, and delivering the pizzas to the tables. We hired another person due to the massive increase, but they only worked part time, so I was still the main one in the front handling it all. As often as I could, I would give the two in the back breaks, since working around the oven and making pizzas was tiring. Especially when we had to also prep all the toppings, sauce, and pizza dough balls before the shift even started.

Gina gave the three of us pay raises due to our increased workload, which I was extremely grateful for.

My parents were leaving in two days, so they'd invited my soon-to-be mates and I over for dinner.

Jong-min tried to insist on cooking, but they wouldn't accept.

After cleaning up the pizzeria like a mad woman, I raced home to shower and change.

As I finished rinsing the shampoo from my hair, the door to my shower opened. Shampoo was in my eyes, so I couldn't see who it was. "We have to wash fast to make it to my parents' on time."

No one responded.

Fire and pain seared into my back as someone stabbed a large knife into me, between my shoulder blade and my spine.

I turned and gaped at Koia. "A gift from him," she said in a weird voice.

I punched her in the chest, sending her flying against the bathroom wall. Her head cracked as it hit the tiled wall and she slid down it, unmoving.

"Help!" I screamed as my legs weakened and I fell to my knees in the shower.

Grant ran inside, saw Koia, and stepped over her to get to me. "Kass! What is Koia doing here? Shit, we need to get that knife out of you."

"I think it's poisoned," I whispered as my breaths came in pants.

Reed ran in and his eyes widened.

"Call Theo," Grant ordered him.

"Is ... she ... dead?" I asked.

Reed squatted and felt for her pulse. He shook his head. "She's alive."

"Why would she attack you like this?" Grant asked.

"I don't know. She said, 'a gift from him,' but I don't know who she could be referring to." I felt pretty confident that I didn't have any enemies that were still alive. Who was this mysterious "him"?

"Where is she?" Theo yelled as she came into the bathroom. Reed had dragged Koia out of the bathroom earlier, but I hadn't wanted to move until we removed the knife from my back. She squatted behind me and inspected the knife. "It's poisoned and there's a spell on it." Narrowing her eyes and using her magic, she focused in silence before she stumbled back. "No!"

"What is it?" Grant asked.

"I'm sorry, Kass. This is my fault," Theo said and swallowed hard. Stepping forward again, she used her magic on my shoulder. "On my order, pull the knife, Grant."

Grant stepped forward and nodded. "Understood."

Closing my eyes and gritting my teeth, I said, "I'm ready."

Theo set her hands on either side of the wound, making me grunt in pain. "Now."

Grant jerked the knife out of my back, tearing a scream from my throat.

Theo used her magic, whispering something as she also put a poultice of some type on the wound as it was closing.

"You should be good in about twenty minutes," she whispered, stood and backed out of the shower.

"Why do you think this is your fault?" I asked.

Grant handed me a towel to wrap around my body as I stood. He kept a hand on my elbow in case I started to fall.

Theo moved into my bedroom, sat on the edge of my bed, and sighed heavily. "That spell, I was able to feel the creator's magic. You can trace a magical signature if you know the person's magic or have the ability to track people by magic. There are several who can do it, but it's a special skill."

She was rambling, but I decided to let her.

"In my former life, I was called a 'Hound' because I was sent to crime scenes to detect magic and then tracked the culprits down. My partner, Roman, was a powerful newbie with some wild ideas and little self-restraint. While hunting down a particularly heinous murderer, we cornered the culprit in a warehouse. My partner found him first and when I got there, he had almost killed him. I had to use my powers to toss him away before he killed the murderer. However, when I flung him away, he landed in a vat of some strange goo. Before I could help him, he sank to the bottom of the vat and when he emerged, he was nearly catatonic. It took me and six healers to heal him enough he could function normally. Whatever was in that vat changed him, and since I had been the one to knock him into it, I became his enemy."

"Wait, so your partner had a true villain origin story?" I asked.

She rolled her eyes, but said, "Yes, and he did become a villain. He not only started going after confirmed criminals, but also suspected criminals. A few of them turned out to be innocent, but he killed them before it could be proven. I was sent to bring him in and it was a really nasty battle. I defeated him, but I was laid up for months after and that was when I decided to retire, and when I started accepting who I really am. He was locked up, but I'd heard a year ago that he escaped. They warned me he might come for me, but after a year, I thought I was safe." She sighed and rubbed her face with her hands. "He must have been watching me, learned you were my friend, and used the spell to send Koia after you."

"So, Koia's not at fault?" Reed asked.

Theo shook her head. "No, she was under compulsion."

"So, your enemy is here and he's just announced his presence by showing us that he can bespell people," Grant summarized.

"Are there limits to how the compulsion works?" I asked. "Would he be able to make me attack you?"

"Roman is a vampire mage," Theo said. "He can make anyone attack anyone else. If there's a hint of dislike, it strengthens the compulsion." She scowled at Koia. "Which is likely why it worked so well on her."

"Does he have to touch you, or how does the compulsion spell work?" Reed asked. "Do you have a picture of him so we can share it with each other?"

"He has to stare into your eyes to get the spell to work. I'll get a photo from my computer files and send it to everyone," Theo said and stood. "And I'm going to start tracking him down."

"This is a trap," I said with certainty. "He gave you a way

to track him down, his magic, knowing you would do that. Why else announce his presence in this way?"

"I know," she said and smiled sadly, "but I have to keep you and everyone I care about safe. This is my sin from the past that I must fix."

"You don't have to do it alone," I reminded her. "That's what we're here for."

She hugged me gently and said, "Thank you, Kass. I don't know what I did to deserve a friend like you, but I'll do what I can to protect you and everyone else. And I won't do it alone. Unlike *someone*, I know it's better to work together with your friends than face a strong enemy alone."

"Wow, way to butter me up to tear me down," I grumbled against her shoulder. "And after I got stabbed for you."

She patted my back where the wound had been. It was fully healed already. "You can take it."

Standing, she stretched and said, "I'm going to my apartment. I'll send the photo and more details about him. What are your plans tonight?"

"We're going to my parents for our farewell dinner," I answered, dropped my towel, and went to the closet to grab clothes. "Do you want to come?"

"No, thanks for the invitation, though. Tell them I hope they have a great trip home. Guys, keep an eye on her, okay?"

"Will do," Reed replied.

"You keep yourself safe, too," Grant ordered her.

"Bye!" she called out.

"Bye!" I called back as I finished dressing. Stepping back into the room, I realized Theo had taken Koia. "Well, not quite the start to the evening I had anticipated, but I suppose our lives are rarely calm."

"And for once, it wasn't your enemy," Grant teased with a smile.

"Come on, we're already late. We need to hurry," Reed said and pushed me out of the room.

"We should grab flowers as an apology on the way," I suggested. "Mom will forgive us if we bring flowers."

Turned out, she was just happy I was safe, but she did put the flowers in a vase in the dining room and kept looking at them throughout the meal.

We ate delicious food, told stories, and cried as we hugged each other for the last time.

"I'm so happy you're mated now," she said. "I was worried about leaving you alone, but you have come very far in your life. We are so proud."

"Thanks, Mom." I hugged her tight one more time before leaving them so they could finish packing.

As I walked out of the house, I felt like a chapter of my life was closing, but I also knew it was the start to another, greater chapter. One with mates who loved me as much as I loved them.

The greatest chapter of my life yet.

As long as we could take out the guy after my best friend, that is.

"Let's go see Silver and my sisters," I said, determined to keep Theo safe. "We need to prepare for yet another battle."

28

Everyone was on high alert with pictures posted everywhere to keep those we cared about safe.

The guys refused to put off the grand re-opening of their new restaurant, SeaZen Palace, despite the potential threat. I understood their reasoning, and was able to request the night off from Gina so I could be there to help them.

If it were my restaurant opening, I would have been a nervous wreck, but the guys were calm and collected as they finished putting out the place settings and prepping all the food.

Since the guys had boasted about the twins' all over the pop music internet boards, they were going to be the main servers for the night. I opted to stay in the back to clean dishes and help with plating food, so I would stay out of the public's eye.

Theo questioned why I wasn't jealous about it, but I explained that these people could come and ogle my men all they wanted without upsetting me, because I knew my men would come home to me that night and every night after. They would smile and dote on the patrons, but that was all they were to them.

I was their soon-to-be mate with the ring on my finger and theirs proved that.

Reed kissed my cheek and rubbed his cheek along my other one. "You are beautiful."

Looking up at him, I arched a brow. "You get into some wolf nip or something?"

He rolled his eyes. "That's not even a thing."

"There's got to be something like catnip for wolves. I'm sure of it. I'll ask Theo. I bet she knows."

Placing hands on either side of my face, he squished my cheeks, making my lips purse, and kissed me roughly. "I love the silly things you say."

"Why are you squishing my face?" I asked.

"So you can't pull back as I do this," he said and licked me from chin to nose.

I spluttered and wiped my face, laughing. "You butt."

"Hey, you two! No shenanigans in the kitchen," Grant snapped. "That's gross and unsanitary."

Reed and I rolled our eyes simultaneously.

"Yes, sir," I said and moved to the door to peek out the window. As I walked by him, I slapped his ass, getting a soft growl from him and a chuckle from Reed.

There were people lined up outside and the twins were smiling smugly.

"Ready?" they asked.

I gave them a thumbs-up in the window.

Grant exhaled harshly. "Well, here we go. Let's hope we prepared enough."

"I think the main issue is going to be the number of patrons wanting to eat here tonight," I commented. "You guys did the test run yesterday with no issues." They had invited all of our friends to come last night as a soft launch and everything went perfectly. Theo had even brought dates with her. Yes, plural. Apparently, the two guys she was currently dating didn't have an issue sharing, and while I wasn't sure about them yet, they clearly cared about Theo.

"Right," Grant said sternly and nodded. "No time for worrying. It's time to focus." As Jong-min sat the first table, Grant filled ice water in glasses and carried them out there.

"I think he's just nervous because we all want this to work and he doesn't want to disappoint the twins," Reed whispered.

"Sorry I'm late," Jong-kyu said as he rushed inside, washed his hands, and put on an apron. "I was spreading word about the opening around town and helping get the line to wrap around the building instead of crossing the street."

"People were trying to line up across the street?" I asked, eyes wide.

He nodded. "My brothers' fans showed up in force. I counted at least fifty people in line."

My mouth dropped. Fifty people all waiting to come eat here.

"That's awesome!" Reed exclaimed.

"There's going to be quite a wait for them," I said and tapped my lips. I put my hand up with a finger in the air. "I got it! Jong-kyu, there are water bottles in the fridge, we were going to use them for us, but why don't you take it to the people who are thirty or more back in line? Let them know that we apologize in advance for their wait time, but we are giving them water to ensure they aren't without anything."

"That's a great idea," he said, shocking me as it was the first time he'd said anything remotely nice about me. He took off the apron and raced into the walk-in refrigerator to do as I'd suggested.

"Oh, the first orders are here. Time to cook!" Reed said excitedly, as the little printer connected remotely to the computer at the waiter stand began printing.

Over the next five hours, there was no time to relax, as the tables stayed filled, and the orders kept coming. One table ordered every item on the menu, and to our surprise, ate it all. Jong-min and Jong-hyun sat in the now empty main room, eyes closed as they relaxed for the first time.

"So, how many pictures did you take tonight?" I asked with a smile.

"Hundreds," Jong-min answered.

"How many times did you get your butt grabbed?" I teased.

"Only once," Jong-hyun replied. "She was in her eighties."

My head fell back as I laughed.

"The opening was definitely a success," Grant said as he looked at the evening's tally. "We just have to hope we can sustain even after the newness has worn off."

"You'd be surprised how many fans are still out there," I said. "There were some making plans to come a few months from now due to financial and personal obligations until then.

I think it's safe to say we'll have business for a few months at least."

"Yes, but it's a year from now that I'm focused on," Grant whispered.

"You all did great tonight," I said. "And while I would love to be part of the permanent staff, I definitely prefer working at the pizza place. Much less stressful."

All of them laughed except Jong-kyu.

"Why did you put Sunday and Monday as days to be closed?" Jong-kyu asked. "You will make more money the more days you are open."

"Because we need a day to relax and a day to spend time with our mate," Jong-min answered and winked at me.

Hearing him call me his mate sent a thrill through my body.

"I already confirmed with Gina that I'll be off those days moving forward," I said and leaned my head on Grant's shoulder since he was nearest me. "She liked the idea of me being available consistently Tuesday through Saturday as those are her busiest days anyway."

"Why two days? You could do that with one day?" Jong-kyu asked.

"You'll understand when you find a mate," Jong-min said. "It's not enough to just be together one day, the same day we're meant to relax. We need a full day to enjoy being in each other's company. With this restaurant, we are going to be busy and likely stressed when we are home and we need to make sure we don't neglect her."

"You're so thoughtful," I said and made a kissy face at him.

"You're different," Jong-kyu whispered.

Jong-min shrugged. "That happens when you find your mate."

"And she melts your cold heart," I added with a wink.

He rolled his eyes, but didn't argue.

The door to the restaurant opened and I said, "We're closed for the day."

When Zara stumbled in, blood streaming down her head and carrying an unconscious Zyra, we all leapt to our feet.

"Help," she whispered. Her eyes rolled up into the back of her head and she fainted.

29

Reed called Silver while Jong-min and Jong-hyun inspected the troll sisters and tried to heal them.

I paced nervously, biting one of my nails. Zara and Zyra were my sworn sisters. We had no blood relation, but had made an oath to be sisters. They were part of my small, found family, and I couldn't bear the thought of losing them. Whoever hurt them was going to pay.

"Silver isn't answering," Reed said and looked at me hesitantly.

"I'm going," I said and headed towards the door. No matter what happened to me, I would give my life to protect my grumpy, adopted father who did more for me than my birth parents ever had.

Grant grabbed my arm, stopping me. "You don't know what's happened. We need to talk to your sisters before—"

"My father may be in trouble," I said, my mouth widening to show more of my teeth. "I am going to go check on him."

"What if Zyran and Zara are injured because Roman bespelled Silver and—"

"I'm going," I said and jerked my arm free. "You can come with me or you can stay, but you will *not* stop me."

Grant scowled at me, clearly fighting with himself on what to do.

"Just go with her," Jong-min said. "We'll call if the twins wake up and we get more information."

"Fine," Grant agreed.

"Love, please stay safe," Jong-hyun said.

"Don't do anything stupid," Jong-min added.

I saluted them and ran out of the restaurant with Grant at my side.

The city was unnervingly quiet, much more so than normal for this time of night.

Grant noticed it, too. "Where is everyone?"

"I was wondering that as well," I admitted. "All that matters is getting to Silver as soon as possible."

"Let me fly us there, it'll be faster," he said, shifting into his dragon form. He grabbed me gently in one of his claws, and flew up into the sky.

I yelped and clung to his foot. Flying was my least preferable mode of transportation.

Though, as I looked below us, it did give me a great vantage point to see the town and it's incredibly empty streets. Where was everyone?

Grant shifted as we were landing, causing me to fall for a brief period of time.

I screamed and flailed my arms, but he caught me a few milliseconds later.

After setting me on my feet outside of the bar, I looked around, taking in the destruction.

There was a huge hole in the wall, tables and chairs broken and scattered inside as well as outside.

Walking into the bar, we found the destruction was even worse.

"What happened here?" Grant asked as he pulled a broken pool stick out of the wall.

"Silver?" I called. "Silver, are you here?" There was some blood on the floor, but not a lot.

Heading around the bar, my eyes widened at the pool of blood there. Hurrying into the back, I threw open his office door and gasped.

Silver sat, bound in chains, his war ax in his left hand, blood dripping down his face from a deep cut on the top of his skull, and a snarl on his face. "I'll kill you all!" he screamed and struggled against the chains. "I will kill every woman in this city!"

My hands went to my mouth and I took a step back, startled to find the kind male, my father figure, in such a state.

Grant pulled me out of the office and shut the door. "He's clearly been put under a spell by Roman. I'm calling Theo."

Wrapping my arms around myself, I took two steps farther back. Fighting against Silver was not a good idea. He was a warrior, after all, and had lots of battle experience. I mean, I had always *wanted* to fight him, but I also didn't want to hurt him.

"Hurry over to Silver's," Grant said into the phone.

Something cracked inside of the office and Silver roared as he kicked the door open.

Standing in the open doorway, Silver spun his ax and smiled. "You should have run, little tiger shark."

Holding out my hands, I said, "You don't want to do this. I'm your daughter, remember? I'm your family. You would never hurt your family."

He scoffed. "Family? You aren't my family. You nor those troll witches."

"He's not himself," Grant reminded me and set a hand on my lower back. "He doesn't mean anything that he's saying. It's just the spell."

I knew that, but it didn't mean that it didn't hurt to hear the words come out of his mouth.

"Out of my way, Dragon, I have no qualms with you," Silver said and made a shooing motion with his hand at Grant.

"You're under a spell, Silver. I don't know if you can break free of it, but you have to try. I know you, and I know if you hurt Kass, you're really only going to hurt yourself. You love her and you don't want to kill her."

"She's cost me thousands of dollars in repairs for all her stunts," he snarled. "For what? A few hundred bucks off of the tourists? Why are you sticking up for her when she costs you so much pain? So many days and nights of torment? I remember you drinking yourself into a stupor because she wouldn't listen to you, wouldn't stay out of trouble, and wouldn't admit her feelings to you."

My breath hitched at the admission from Silver.

"That was over a year ago," Grant said. "We have worked through our issues and we're sworn to be mated."

Silver's eyes widened. "Mated?"

Grant and I nodded.

Silver threw his head back, set a hand on his stomach, and laughed so loud I flinched back. "You're actually going to agree to be mated to ... this *thing*? You lot really have lost your mind. I've seen the girls who throw themselves at you. You could do so much better."

"Listen here, old man," I snapped and bared my teeth. "I love you, but I'm tired of your mouth. Also, I'm pretty sure you hurt my sisters, your adoptive daughters, and I think it's time to shut you up and make you pay for the pain you caused them."

He gripped his ax and smiled viciously. "Try it. I've killed hundreds of beings during my lifetime."

My anger ebbed a bit as I softened my voice and said, "I know. I know how much it hurts you to have all those deaths on your hands. That's why I know you don't actually want to kill me. If you did, you would feel like my death had been the final piece to tarnish your soul, fully beyond repair or redemption."

His ax dropped a bit, giving me the distraction that I needed.

Jumping forward, I slammed my shoulder into his chest while simultaneously grabbing the wrist of the arm that held his ax. With a sharp twist, I snapped his wrist bone.

He punched me in the side with his other hand as he roared in pain and the ax fell to the ground.

Grant kicked the ax away so Silver couldn't pick it back up.

Jumping away from him, I let my scales flow over most of my body and shifted partially, including a tail. Dancing on the balls of my feet, I held my fists up, punching the air in quick jabs, and smiled wide. "What's wrong, old man? Out of shape?"

"Kass, don't taunt him," Grant growled as he also shifted.

"Impudent uncultured child," Silver growled.

"Grumpy old codger," I bit back while smiling wide. I sure hoped he remembered this when the spell was lifted. It would entertain me for decades to come. I was fairly certain he wouldn't look me in the eye for at least a week after the spell was removed and he retained his memories. Memories of me beating his ass and talking so much shit he couldn't respond.

He tried to punch me, but I leaned out of the way of the jab and hit him in the stomach with an upper cut. He made a satisfying, "oomph," from the hit.

I danced on my toes, throwing short jabs to his face and stomach, being careful of his unbroken tusk so I didn't cut myself.

He roared in anger, darting forward to grab my hair, and jerked me forward as he headbutted me.

Stars filled my vision and I stumbled back, dizzy and disoriented. Shark skulls were made of cartilage and thus not strong against headbutts by bone skulled ogres.

Grant pulled me back as Silver tried to attack me again, and punched Silver in the chest, causing him to slide back through the puddle of blood and hit his back against the bar top.

Grant pushed me around the bar top, keeping himself between Silver and me.

"You always talk big, but you can never back it up," Silver said as he shook his head, clearly disoriented.

"Please, old man, you don't know what you're talking about. I put it down when necessary and this little fight is not requiring a tenth of my focus." Sure, I was dizzy, my head hurt, and I might have been taken out if Grant hadn't intervened, but shit talking was one of my love languages.

Theo burst into the bar, panting, sweating, and for the first time, not wearing a wig. "Where is he?"

Grant and I pointed.

"Another woman to kill," Silver snarled.

Theo sighed, marched forward, and slapped her hand against Silver's cheek. "Shut up, you crochety, old, grumpy male."

Silver slumped forward and passed out on the bar top.

30

Just to be safe, we tied Silver up, unsure if when he woke, he would still be bespelled. Grant carried him back to the restaurant, where my sisters had been healed enough to wake and tell us what had happened.

As I had expected, they'd gotten injured fighting Silver, trying not to truly hurt their adopted father.

Neither remembered seeing Roman, but he had obviously been at the bar to be able to put the spell on Silver.

"That means he's in the city," I said, "which means we can track him down and kill him."

"It's not that simple, Kass," Theo said with a sigh. "He's extremely powerful. I don't know if I'll be able to defeat him even with my powers."

Zara said, "If we combine our powers, devise a plan, we should be able to take him down."

Zyra nodded. "With enough force, any skull will crack."

Leave it to my troll warrior sister to say something so simplistic, but valid.

While it seemed possible to come up with a plan that utilized all our abilities, Theo's fear of him made me worried, even with so many of us.

Silver woke with a groan. He looked down and asked, "Why am I tied up?" He looked around and asked, "Is this another surprise party?"

Remembering the time we had tried to throw him a party that had caused him to lash out in shock at our yelled "surprise" made me smile.

"You don't remember me kicking your ass?" I asked with a wide, innocent smile.

"So, that wasn't a dream?" he sighed and looked at the troll sisters. "Are you okay?"

Zyra smiled. "Thankfully, you're slower in your old age."

He snarled, but then sighed and shook his head. "I failed to protect my daughters. I am sorry."

I patted his shoulder. "It's alright, Pops! I had fun fighting you." Bending down, I untied him. "We tied you up in case you were still under the spell's influence."

"Smart move," he said with a nod. Once he was freed, he took turns hugging me, Zyra, and Zara. "I'm proud of you three. Even if I am slower in my old age, you did well against me." He looked at me. "It's worrying that you're so susceptible to headbutts. You need to remember that."

I waved his words away. "I'm fine. It barely hurt."

He scoffed, but didn't say more.

"Perhaps it's time to involve the hunters," I said as I turned back to Theo. "I have the contact info for that one hunter who gave me his business card when Bastian was here."

Theo scowled and clenched her fists.

"I know you hate them, but this is out of our control at this point," Jong-min said. "What if they get Kass? You have a soft spot for her that will likely cause you to get injured just as Zara and Zyra got injured fighting Silver."

Theo rubbed her temples. "Fine. Fine. Call him, Kass."

I pulled out my phone and stepped out of the restaurant's front door. A second later, Jong-hyun joined me.

"I don't want you alone," he explained. "We don't know where he is right now and I'd rather not have to fight you."

I smiled and asked, "Afraid I might bite an arm off?"

He nodded, completely serious. "Yes, actually."

Chuckling, I dialed the hunter's number and waited for him to answer.

"Who is this?" he answered.

"This is Kass, the shark shifter you gave your card to when Bastian was here. We have a problem."

There was a shuffling sound and I could hear a door close before he asked, "What kind of problem?"

I filled him in on what I knew and at the end, he said, "We've been searching for Roman for years. You're telling me that he is here, in our city, at this very moment?"

"Yep," I replied. "He is bespelling people to try to kill Theo's friends. Can you help us?"

"Let me call my superiors and I'll call you back. Whatever you do, do not engage with Roman. Theo is correct, he is incredibly powerful."

"Well, if he shows up here, I don't know that we can do much except fight, so you better make that a quick call."

He grumbled something that sounded like, "pushy

shark," but I couldn't be certain since he hung up immediately afterwards.

We walked back inside and locked the door behind us, just in case.

"What did he say?" Theo asked.

"He's calling his superiors and he'll call me back." Sitting down at the table beside her, I patted her hand. "Don't worry, we're not going to let you face him alone."

"That's sort of what I'm worried about," she said. "I don't think I can fight him with all of you here."

"Aw, you're worried about me? That's so sweet," I teased and kissed her cheek.

She pushed my face away, but I saw her smile for a brief second, which meant … goal achieved!

Her phone rang and she walked away to answer it. After a few minutes she said, "My, um, boyfriends are on their way here. I figured it's better to gather everyone here to better protect you all."

"So, you did go with the multiple partner option. Good for you!" I said and gave her a thumbs up.

Her cheeks reddened and she flipped her hair over her shoulder and turned her face to try to hide it. "Shut up." She sat down beside me again with her arms crossed over her chest.

"How many are you going to end with? Four? Seventeen? Knowing you and how extra, I mean, awesome you are, you'll end up with like two dozen."

She smacked my arm. "Brat."

Resting my head on her shoulder, I smiled up at her. "I'm happy you've found people. Honestly, I was starting to get worried you'd be alone forever and you are too awesome to be alone forever."

"I was getting worried too," she muttered. "I thought with how much more accepting the world is with transgender people now that I wouldn't have as many issues, but ..." She sighed loudly. "It still is an issue for a lot of people. I dated a few, but when they realized I was trans ... let's just say one particular break up almost became a physical fight."

"Who?" I demanded. "Who dared to try to fight you? I'll tear their arms off."

She draped her arm around my shoulders and squeezed. "They're not worth your time, Kass. Besides, I may or may not have cursed him, so there's no need for you to tear his arm off."

Theo loved cursing people, though she normally only did it for a short period of time. Just long enough to get her point across to them that they shouldn't mess with a witch.

My phone rang at the same time that someone knocked on the door.

The guys all approached the door cautiously.

"Hello?" I answered.

"It's my guys," Theo said as she approached the door.

"Where are you currently?" the hunter asked.

"My pack's restaurant. It used to be my parent's restaurant."

"Yes, I know which it is. Stay there. We are on our way."

"Understood," I said.

Jong-min, Jong-hyun, Grant, and Reed stepped back at Theo's declaration, but kept focused on the doors still.

Theo pulled open the door, a smile on her face.

As the door opened, a huge explosion sent us all flying backwards.

31

Coughing with ringing so loud in my ears that I was dizzy, I slowly sat up.

"Kass! Kass!" Reed called out, his voice far away and distorted by the ringing in my ears.

There were so many sounds and ringing and ... pain.

"Kass! Get up!" Grant bellowed. His yell was immediately followed by a scream of pain.

Grant was in pain?

Not just him.

I could hear other cries of pain.

Forcing my eyes open, I took slow, even breaths as I surveyed my surroundings.

The front door of the restaurant was blown apart and now a gaping hole. There was shattered glass all over the restaurant from the front windows that had been on either side of the door before it had exploded.

Theo was outside on the street, magic swirling around her in a dazzling and almost blinding display. Her wig was gone and her short, natural hair stuck out like she'd been electrocuted. Her eyes glowed white as she shielded herself against magic blasts being shot at her.

Grant and Reed stood just outside what used to be the front door, bodies shifted into warrior forms, but both were not fighting or even attempting to join the fight.

Where were the twins? I couldn't see them, so maybe they were outside.

Zara bent down beside me, blood dripping down her face, and started using magic to heal me. "Are you okay, Sister?"

"I've been better," I wheezed as I struggled to sit up.

Silver grabbed a chair nearby, smashed it against the ground, and spun the now splintered chair leg in his hand like an ax. "Stay down if you're too injured to fight, Daughters."

"I can't be outshone by an old bastard like you," I breathed and tried to stand, but my knees wobbled and I fell.

Zyra put her hands in my armpits, lifted me to my feet, and slapped a hand on my shoulder. "That's my sister. Let's go show this enemy what happens when they mess with our family."

Zara sighed. "How about a little rage? Will that help?"

"Rage?" I asked.

She smiled. "You're not the only one who has been practicing and trying to improve their abilities." Exhaling, she held her hands out like cupping a ball and a red light began to glow between them. "I'm going to give you a bit of rage to help you fight."

"Oh, *rage*! Yes, please! I'll take a double helping." I smiled and clapped my hands together.

She made the light grow larger and instructed, "You three touch the light."

Zyra, Silver, and I reached out and touched the red light.

Immediately, a burning rage exploded within me.

I screamed, threw my head back, and shifted into a shark-woman warrior form complete with a tail, fin, and a wider head to accommodate more teeth. "Blood!" I screamed. "I need blood!"

Zyra growled loudly beside me. "Let's hunt!"

We ran outside, Silver right behind us, and before anyone could react, the three of us began attacking Roman and the two goblins standing on either side of him.

He had been so focused on Theo that he'd not realized we were close and battle ready.

I punched him in the face with knuckles covered in my shark scales that immediately sliced his skin apart.

Zyra had a short sword and cut into his chest. Silver swung the chair leg and it shattered on impact with Roman's head.

Roman stumbled a step back, but raised his hand and used a spell to knock us all back.

There were three others helping Roman fight Theo from a distance away. They appeared to be witches as they looked human and were flinging magic spells with abandon, but I didn't recognize them.

My feet bumped into something as I slid backwards and when I glanced down, I realized it was Damien, the orca shifter that Theo had been dating and next to him was Tristan, the dolphin shifter Theo had dated. Were they her boyfriends? Was she really dating an orca and a dolphin?

Part of me was hurt, but I blamed that on the rage still boiling within me, so I pushed those feelings aside.

I glanced at her and saw the fear in her eyes as she looked at me and the two men at my feet. Was she afraid I would hurt them? I may not like their kind in general, but I would never harm someone she cared about. Gritting my teeth together to quell my rage a bit, I quickly looped an arm around each of the unconscious males, and ran towards the restaurant with them.

Grant's eyes widened when he saw something behind me. He exhaled a huge breath of fire, which I ducked under as I continued to carry Theo's men. I presumed he was breathing fire at Roman or his minions to keep my back safe.

I ran into the kitchen and put the two unconscious men on the floor. Inspecting them, I saw no huge wounds, so I left them. Most shifters would regain consciousness not too long after being knocked out thanks to the fast healing. I just hoped they did it sooner than later as we could use as many fighters as possible.

Heading back out, I realized Jong-min and Jong-hyun were completely missing. "Where are the twins?" I demanded as I walked up behind Reed and Grant.

"Jong-kyu teleported them away. They were severely injured," Reed explained.

Exhaling, I said, "I hope he can heal them. I'm going back into the fray. Care to join me?"

"We can't move," Grant growled. "There's a spell on us, keeping us rooted to this spot."

Why would he keep Grant and Reed stuck, but not me?

"Be safe," Reed ordered me.

I winked. "Yes, sir."

Silver and Zyra had killed the two goblins and were trying to fight the witches, but the witches were doing a good job keeping them back. Zara had come outside and was fighting against them as well, trying to give Silver and Zyra opportunities to get closer.

Running over to Theo, I asked, "What do you need?"

"More power," she said, her jaw clenched. Her top was torn, exposing her flat, bare chest beneath and a deep gash across one side.

"How can I help with that? Can you use some of my power? Can I give you energy or something?"

Roman started to move closer, but Theo sent a wall of wind that pushed him back and sliced into his cheek, making him hiss in pain.

"He's so strong, Kass," she whispered and her lip trembled.

I slapped her across the face hard, making her face swing to the side from the impact.

Roman blinked in disbelief and lowered his hands, stopping the attack he had been about to use.

Theo blinked tears out of her eyes and her lips trembled as she looked at me.

"Stop whining and acting afraid! You're one hundred times the witch he is. You were one of the most terrifying witches of the Hunters Association. You defeated dozens, probably hundreds, of beings. You faced years of ridicule when you came out as transgender, but you did it with a smile on your face, as you were able to finally live your life as the person you always knew you were. What's scarier? This douche nozzle or the night you told your parents you had changed not just your name, but also your pronouns?"

Her lips stopped trembling and curved upwards in a smile. She threw her head back and laughed. As her head dropped back down, she wrapped her arms around me. "I love you, Kass."

I patted her back. "I love you, too. Now, tell me what to do so we can kill this mother fucker."

Releasing me, she faced Roman and said, "Time to end this."

Behind Theo, I saw the hunter I'd called and another man in a matching cloak running towards us. "The hunters arrived," I whispered.

"Tell them to loop around and attack from the rear. I'm going to send a barrage of attacks at him. If we can keep those three witches Silver and the troll sisters are fighting busy, we have a good chance of taking him down. The hunters just need to wait for an opening."

"You got it, boss." I winked at her and ran to relay the plan to the hunters.

32

The hunters stopped when they saw me approaching and waited for me to meet them.

"What's the situation?" the hunter I recognized asked.

"What's your name?" I asked. "I can't call you 'hunter' since there are two of you."

"Antoine," he answered. He pointed to the one next to him. "Phil."

"Okay, Antoine and Phil. I'm Kass. Those people over there are mostly my family and friends, but the three witches and the crazy man Roman are our enemies. They blew a hole in the wall of the restaurant and they're trying to kill Theo. She said that you can sneak around so that you can attack from behind to try to catch him off guard. I think we need to come at him from multiple directions at once."

"We heard from our Director and they're sending more people, but they won't be here for about an hour," Antoine said as he looked beyond me at the fight going on.

I needed to get back to help, to ensure Theo didn't lose.

"Do you have any potions?" I asked.

Phil pulled out a small bottle from his pocket and held it out. "Stamina," he said in a deep, stony voice.

"Thanks," I chirped, spun and ran towards Theo.

She noticed me coming and created a shield to keep Roman's attacks from hitting me. "What are you doing, crazy?" she hissed.

Opening the bottle, I shoved it between her lips. "Drink."

She tilted her head back and swallowed the liquid. Immediately, her eyes widened and the darkness beneath her eyes lessened. "Whoa," she whispered. "That was a potent stamina potion."

"You can thank Phil the hunter," I explained. "How is it going?"

I looked over at Roman who was glaring at us and trying to hit us with ice shards, but they disintegrated on impact of her shield.

"We're at a stalemate," she muttered. "I can't get past his defenses and he can't get past mine. We're pretty much going to continue until one of us runs out of stamina or magic."

"Well, you just got a stamina boost, so hopefully it's not going to be you."

She sighed. "This is the most annoying fight I've ever been part of."

Behind Roman, I saw the two hunters approaching.

"They're behind him now," I said. "I'm going to distract him so you and the hunters can attack and hopefully catch him off guard."

"How are you going to distract him?" she asked.

I winked. "You'll see."

Did I have a plan? Nope! But I was the queen of going with the flow. So, that was my plan.

Taking a breath, I refocused on the rage simmering inside of me from Zara's spell. It resurfaced and I shifted into my shark warrior form again. Letting my mouth open wide to show off my full-sized shark teeth, I squatted down, flexed my muscles, and sprinted away from Theo and at Roman.

He tried to hit me with some ice shards, but I zig-zagged, dashed towards the restaurant, ran along the sidewalk a bit, then ran towards him again.

As he turned to fire off a spell at me, Antoine drew his sword and jumped in an arc to try to cut into Roman's shoulder.

Roman rolled to the side, stopping him from using the fire spell.

It gave Theo a chance to shoot off her own fire spell that hit him squarely in the chest, sending him flying back through the air to slam against the side of a building.

Was that it? Had we defeated him? It seemed too easy. For someone who was supposed to be a crazy strong villain, he hadn't put up that much of a fight.

Looking at Theo, I saw her squatted down to relax for a moment while we waited to see what would happen.

"Kass!" Antoine yelled.

As I turned, an electric green magical whip wrapped around my midsection, jerking me up and towards the building where Roman had fallen.

Screaming in pain, I almost immediately blacked out.

Sharks were very susceptible to electric shocks and the amount coursing through me was almost enough to kill me.

My limp body was thrown through the air, but I couldn't open my eyes, let alone try to stop my fall.

I hit something solid and warm that smelled like Jong-min.

The warm thing vibrated against my head.

Ringing in my ears lessened and external noise increased.

"Can you hear me yet?" Jong-min asked.

"Min?" I whispered and realized that my voice was hoarse. Was it from me screaming while being electrocuted?

"Can you open your eyes?" he asked.

I tried, but failed, and it hurt to even try. "Hurts," I hissed.

"I'm trying to heal you, so stay still," he ordered gruffly.

How could he be mad at me? I didn't do anything wrong.

"He's not mad at you," Jong-hyun whispered and I felt his hand on mine. "He's mad that you are hurt."

Had I said that out loud? Was I speaking and didn't realize it? Should I stop talking so that I didn't declare that I desperately wanted to be the filling to a twin sandwich again? It had been months since I'd last had that chance and I was craving it.

"She must feel fine if she's saying all that," Jong-min mumbled.

"Stop talking," Jong-hyun ordered. "You're injured and we're trying to heal you."

"Where were you?"

"Our younger brother teleported us away," Jong-min said and growled. He also muttered something under his breath that sounded like it was a bad word.

"We're sorry that we weren't here to help," Jong-hyun whispered and stroked his thumb across the back of my hand.

"What happened after the tentacle snatched me?" I asked and started trying to open my eyes again.

"Whip, not tentacle," Jong-min said. "Stop talking."

"Why don't I hear fighting?" I asked. "What happened?"

"He tried to use you as a hostage, but then threw you at Theo. While you were flying through the air, he used a spell at the same time as Theo."

My eyes finally opened and I saw Theo standing next to a bloody puddle. The two hunters stood nearby, phones to their ears.

"She obliterated him," Jong-min whispered, "using an illegal spell."

"An illegal spell?" I asked.

"It was the only way to save you. If she hadn't used it, you were going to be destroyed by Roman's spell, also an illegal one," Jong-min explained.

Tristan and Damien ran out of the restaurant and over to Theo, checking her over for injuries and hugging her.

She cried as she hugged them.

Pushing at Jong-min's hands, I tried to get to my feet, but they resisted.

"I need to get up. I need to talk to Antoine."

"Who is Antoine?" Jong-hyun asked with a bit of a snarl as he helped me to my feet.

"The hunter," I explained. My legs wobbled. Looking up at Jong-hyun I asked, "Uppies?", raised my arms up, and wiggled my fingers.

Jong-min scooped me up in a bridal carry and walked me

over to Antoine. "My mate wants to speak to you," he snapped.

Antoine hung up his phone and asked, "How are you feeling?"

"I've been better. Now's not the time for that. Are you going to report Theo?"

He scowled. "I have to."

"No you don't," I said quickly. "You could say you didn't see what happened in the smoke. You could let her live out her life instead of going to prison."

"She used an illegal spell—"

"To save us all," I snapped and hopped out of Jong-min's arms. "You know Roman was about to use an illegal spell as well. One that likely would have destroyed all of us."

His lips thinned.

"We are obligated to report what we see," Phil said as he came to join us.

"You're going to send her to jail because you guys were too incompetent to find Roman before he attacked us?" I asked and folded my arms across my chest.

Phil and Antoine flinched.

"Perhaps we could alter our report slightly," Antoine said with a loud sigh. "There was a lot of smoke and I was watching you fly through the air instead of focusing on the target."

I hugged Antoine and kissed his cheek, ignoring the growl I heard behind me from Jong-min. "Thank you."

"You owe me one, Shark," he muttered as he walked away.

"Ditto," Phil said.

"Okay, bye! Thanks for coming!" I yelled and waved as they walked over to Theo, Damien, and Tristan.

"You sure you're okay with owing a hunter?" Grant asked as he and Reed joined us.

"I'd rather owe them then see my best friend go to prison for the rest of her life." Especially when this was the first time I had seen her with men who she seemed to truly be happy with.

How could I not do whatever was within my capabilities to let her continue dating them and see if this was her happily ever after?

I had found mine, and if I could help my friend in finding hers, I would do whatever that meant, including owing a favor to a terrifying member of an organization that used to hunt Theo and I.

Maybe I could make Antoine my friend and he could protect us from future hunter interference?

Yeah! That sounded like a great idea.

"What are you thinking about?" Jong-min asked and tapped my forehead with his finger. "You've got that, 'I have a crazy scheme' face on. It worries me."

"I never come up with crazy schemes," I said with a huff and spun away from them to head towards the destroyed restaurant.

"Lied the pool shark shifter woman," Grant whispered behind me.

"Said the card shark dragon shifter man," I countered.

"Ha!" Reed laughed. "She got you there."

"You're all a bunch of sharks," Theo said as she walked

over to hug me. "And I think you're great, serrated teeth and all."

"So, going to introduce me to your boyfriends?"

She flinched and chuckled awkwardly as she stepped back. "Um, Damien and Tristan, meet my pool shark bestie and her shifter card shark men."

"Uh, what?" Damien asked.

Theo and I burst into laughter and hugged each other as we laughed until we cried.

Silver, Zara, and Zyra joined us after handing over the tied-up witches that had been assisting Roman.

"What's so funny?" Silver asked.

"We really are a rag tag group of people," I said as I looked around. "And I wouldn't have it any other way."

33

It only took a week to rebuild the restaurant and Silver's bar and replace all the items that had been destroyed, thanks to help from the community.

Luckily, business was even more popular at the restaurant after the twins' fans heard they'd almost died. That exaggeration had caused many to up their plans for visiting. Jongkyu was punished by the twins for teleporting them away and preventing them from helping me by being forced to serve food, which caused an uproar in the community when the fans learned there was another brother. He gained his own group of fans who started coming to the restaurant and had numbers slipped to him every single night.

He wouldn't admit it, but we could tell his smile as he floated around the restaurant, serving the women was genuine. We had a betting pool for how long it would be before he was mated. Due to his popularity and the number of dates he started going on, he got his own apartment, which gave us back our privacy.

Theo had cried and hugged Antoine when he told her they weren't going to report her use of the illegal spell. The hunter had blushed furiously and it wasn't long before her two boyfriends became three.

My plan to make friends with Antoine to keep hunters away from us became much easier after that.

Since they'd altered their report, Antoine and Phil got credit for bringing Roman down, but Theo said she preferred it that way. The less her name was in the news, the better.

Zara, Zyra, Silver, and I had a family dinner where we teased Silver endlessly about being bested by his daughters. He'd taken it well and it was a night I would remember for the rest of my life.

Even though we felt certain most of our enemies were gone now, we started having weekly training sessions. Even Theo and her men joined in once a month.

Things were settling into a calm recurring cycle of work, training, and spending time with the people I loved.

On a Sunday afternoon a few weeks after the battle, I lay on the couch eating snacks and watching a silly comedy show, when all four of my men walked into the room with me.

Jong-min turned off the television and stepped in front of it.

"Hey! I was watching that," I protested.

Grant squatted down in front of me, slid his hands beneath my back and under my knees, and scooped me up into his arms. Without a word, he carried me upstairs to my room where he placed me on my bed and stepped back so I could see all four of them lined up just inside my door.

"What's going on?" I asked nervously. Had I done something? Was I in trouble?

The four of them started stripping their clothes off and my mouth went dry.

So much delicious skin and muscles on display. I couldn't think right with so many rippling muscles in front of me.

Jong-min pointed at me and ordered, "Strip."

I scrambled and frantically pulled off my clothes, dumping them on the ground without thought.

Jong-min stalked closer, dropped to his knees before me at the edge of the bed, and slid his hands up my thighs. "We're sorry that we've been so busy with the restaurant. We're sorry we ever let this get delayed, but it's time."

"Time?" I asked, swallowing hard and leaning into his touch as his hands stroked up my arms.

"Time for us to officially become your mates," he said and placed gentle kisses around my face.

Oh. Oh!

"Yes, please!" I shouted and scooted back on the bed until I was in the center of it, then lay down, held out my hands, and made grabby motions.

Grant chuckled and launched himself at me, landing on his hands and knees over me. "Glad to know there's no hesitation in your desire to be mated to us."

I shook my head. "Zero hesitation. Mate me, please."

Reed groaned and gripped his erection. "I don't think I've ever heard a sexier phrase."

Grant nudged my legs apart, bent over, and latched onto my clit with a hard suction that made my legs jerk and a gasp escape my mouth. His tongue slid between my already slick folds and he moaned as he thrust his tongue into me.

I gripped his hair, urging him to go faster and he complied.

Reed and Jong-hyun dropped to their knees on either side of the bed, bending over to kiss and suck on my breasts.

Jong-min stood at the end of the bed, stroking himself while he enjoyed the scene.

Grant slid two fingers inside of me, curved just slightly to hit that delicious spot inside as he pumped them in and out of me while he continued to lick and suck my clit in the way he knew I loved.

It wasn't long before my orgasm exploded out of me and I screamed in ecstasy, my entire body convulsing in pleasure.

Grant wiped his mouth with the back of his hand, straightened, and pressed against my entrance. "Are you ready, Kass?"

I nodded vigorously. "Yes. More than ready."

He thrust into me and Reed and Jong-hyun stepped back to let Grant dropp his upper body down, a hand on either side of my head as he thrust into me and placed gentle nips and kisses along my neck and shoulders.

While our lovemaking sessions always varied, this one was definitely the most unique. I could feel the difference in his intention and it made me even wetter than usual.

As my orgasm built from his powerful thrusts and the teasing bites, I felt the intense urge for his mating bite. I wanted, no needed his mark.

"Mark me," I begged. "Please, Grant."

He bit into the side of my neck as his pace increased,

growling in the back of his throat, and a sizzle of pain rolled through me as the mark was placed. I cried out as the strongest orgasm I'd yet to receive rolled through me and I felt not just my pleasure, but Grant's as well as he found his own release.

He licked at his mark and every lick caused aftershocks of pleasure to ripple through me. With a soft kiss to my cheek, he withdrew and took a warm washcloth from Reed to clean me. "Mine," he said as he stared into my eyes.

I smiled and nodded. "Mine."

He smiled and nodded back.

Reed crawled onto the bed, placing gentle kisses along my arm as he made his way over to center himself between my legs. "Do you need a break or—"

I thrust my hips up, impaling myself on his cock and smiled at his shocked face. "No breaks. I want your mark on me."

Reed growled happily, put his hands beneath my hips, and raised them to get a better angle as he pounded into me at an unrelenting pace.

Just as my orgasm was about to crescendo, he bit down on my neck, just above where Grant had marked me, and placed his mark.

Stars danced across my vision and I forgot how to breathe for a moment as all of the sensations, mine and his, flowed through me.

He dropped to his elbows above me, panting. "I ... I didn't think it was going to be so intense."

"Tell me about it," I said and chuckled.

Reed kissed my lips tenderly before climbing off the bed.

Jong-min held out a glass of water. "Drink."

"Yes, sir," I said with a smile before chugging the water. I hadn't realized how thirsty I was until I started drinking.

Once I finished it, he turned to Jong-hyun and said, "Lie on the bed."

Jong-hyun obeyed, lying next to me with a soft smile that was at complete odds with his hard erection.

"Kass, on top of him," Jong-min ordered.

"Don't have to tell me twice," I muttered and started to climb atop Jong-hyun, facing him. I slowly sank down until he was fully sheathed within me, moaning at the feel of him.

Jong-hyun gripped my hips and moaned as well.

Jong-min crawled onto the bed, his warm hands stroking my back and sending delightful chills up my spine. "We're going to take you and mark you at the same time, okay?"

A twin sandwich! I was going to be the middle of a delicious twin sandwich.

"Yes," I said and nodded vigorously.

"Good girl," he praised in a soft whisper in my ear that made me moan and squirm atop Jong-hyun, causing his grip to tighten.

"Now, ride him until you're about to orgasm, but stop before you do," he ordered.

"I don't know that I like this plan, but okay," I whispered as I placed my hands on Jong-hyun's chest and started moving, rising up until just before he could slip out of me and falling back down with a hard slap of skin.

Jong-min reached around me, one hand stroking my clit and the other kneading one of my breasts.

"Here," Reed gave Jong-min a bottle of lube and he

released my breast to apply some to himself, stroking himself as he stroked me.

"So beautiful," Jong-hyun said. "I could watch you ride me all day."

"Close," I panted, my fingertips digging slightly into his chest.

Jong-min pushed my back down until my chest was pressed to Jong-hyun's, then he slowly began to enter me, giving me time to accommodate his girth. "Slow, deep breaths," he ordered me and I realized I was holding my breath.

We'd done this before, but it had been a while, so it took a bit of time before they were both fully inside of me, but once they were, I moaned and felt myself flexing around the both of them, stretching me to my fullest.

"I'm going to go slow and easy until you're more relaxed," he said in my ear. "You stay still while we pleasure you."

As if I was going to say no to that!

"You're so beautiful," Jong-hyun whispered, "especially when you're taking us both so well." He kneaded my breasts while Jong-min and he moved in and out of me faster and faster, matching each other somehow without speaking.

Reaching down, I rubbed my clit and gently nipped Jong-hyun's chest.

"Min," Jong-hyun moaned.

Jong-min said, "Okay, my queen, it's time."

I nodded in understanding as they moved even faster. My fingers moved faster and in an explosion of stars, I screamed at the same time they both moaned my name. The three of us orgasmed together and the brothers bit into the same side of my neck, the opposite side from Grant and Reed, with Jong-min's above Jong-hyun.

Closing my eyes, I gasped as I felt all four of their emotions, all four of their love and adoration, swirling within me.

Finally. I finally had my mates' marks on me.

I was mated. Five years ago, I would never have believed it.

The guys took me into the shower, washing me and gently cleaning the marks on my neck with happy smiles on their faces.

"I love you," I said as they rinsed my hair.

"I love you, too," they all said simultaneously.

The smile on my face was so wide, I thought it might split, but that was fine with me. No matter what happened, I had my mates, my pack, and we would face everything together.

34

"Where are you taking me?" I demanded. My hands were tied and I had a blindfold on, preventing me from seeing where I was.

The blindfold was removed and I blinked against the bright, harsh lights a moment as my eyes adjusted.

"Congratulations!" Silver, Zara, Zyra, Gina, Theo, Tristan, Damien, and Antoine shouted. More congratulations were shouted from the regulars and from Tonka as he came inside to join us as well.

Silver's bar had been decorated with silver streamers and a "Congratulations!" banner.

"What's this?" I asked as I looked at my mates who had kidnapped me here.

"It's your congratulations on being mated party," Theo explained as she came over and hugged me. "We knew you wouldn't throw one yourself and so we decided to throw one for you. I'm so happy for you."

I hugged her back and laughed. "You're right, I wouldn't

have thrown one for myself. Thank you." I peeked around her at the three men staring at her butt and said, "Seems like your party may not be far off."

She blushed and smacked my arm playfully. "Stop it. We've just started dating, mating is far off."

"That's what I said, too," I reminded her with a smirk.

The guys drifted away from me, chatting with everyone and getting drinks from Silver.

Zara and Zyra came over and handed Theo and I drinks. The drink glittered and swirled in a hypnotic pattern.

"Don't worry, there is no pixie dust lite in there," Zara said with a wink.

"A toast, to our sister and her happiness," Zyra shouted and raised her glass in the air.

"To Kass and her happiness!" Zara shouted.

Everyone in the bar cheered and toasted as well.

I was pretty sure my face was going to hurt tomorrow from smiling too much tonight.

"You sure you don't want us to try to help with your fertility?" Zara asked.

"I've been doing research on it and there are spells and potions that can help," Theo added.

I shook my head. "Thank you, but we've spoken about it and at this time, we don't want children. If that changes, I'll let you all know, but as of right now, we don't foresee kids in our future."

"One Kass is enough trouble for us," Jong-min said as he came up behind me, draped his arm around my shoulders, and kissed my cheek.

"True that," Theo teased. "I'm glad I can pass her off to

you guys. I'm exhausted. I think she took ten years off my life."

I stuck my tongue out at her.

She whispered something and a flower appeared on my tongue making me cough and wildly scrub it off.

Everyone laughed as I chased her around the bar, Theo included.

After getting a good pinch in, I went to the bar and sat to face Silver. "You ever think this day was going to come?"

He smiled. "I hoped you would find your people, and while I was hesitant to like them at first, they really proved themselves and their love."

"Yeah, they are hopelessly in love with me," I agreed with a laugh.

"It's hard not to love you," he said as he made me another drink.

"Except when I'm pissing off your patrons and causing damage to your bar."

He laughed and said, "Even then, I was still filled with pride. You were able to play those men so easily and made so much money. It was hard to believe, but I watched you do it again and again."

I blinked in shocked silence. He'd never said he was proud of my pool shark habits before.

"Are you dying?" I asked.

He rolled his eyes. "I realized after almost losing you and the girls that life is short and I need to tell you three how I feel more often. I want you to know that I am proud of you and am so happy to be part of your life."

Tears sprang to my eyes and I said, "I'll take that drink now."

He smiled and put the drink on the bar top in front of me.

"I challenge you!" Theo shouted.

I spun on the barstool to face her with an arched brow. "What kind of challenge?"

"Me versus you at pool," she said.

My eyes widened. "You're challenging *me* to pool? Me? The ultimate pool shark shark?"

She nodded. "I've been practicing and I'm certain I can defeat you now."

Hopping off the stool, I smiled and said, "What are the terms?"

"If I win, you have to cook us dinner at the restaurant," she said. "If you win, we'll cook you dinner at my place."

"Wager accepted," I said and smiled. She was so going down.

"Don't break anything!" Silver ordered us as we headed to the pool tables.

I raised my hand to let him know that we had heard him.

Once inside the room, I went to the wall where the pool cues were, clicked the button to open the secret compartment, and pulled out my custom cue. The stick was black with silver swirls and a tiger shark in the center. It was perfectly weighted and had cost quite a bit of money, but I loved it and used it every chance I could get.

"Coin toss for break?" Theo asked.

I shook my head. "You challenged me, so I get to break. Don't act like you don't know the rules."

She laughed. "Fine. Go ahead and break."

While she racked the balls, her boyfriends and my mates came into the room. I thought they were going to watch us, but instead, they split up to have games of their own.

Jong-min took the table next to ours and kissed my cheek as he waited for Antoine to rack the balls on their table. "You look beautiful," he whispered. "Being mated suits you."

"Why thank you."

"Also, you better win this," he whispered and kissed me again.

"What did you guys bet?" I asked.

"You'll have to wait to find out after I win," he said and moved to start the game.

"Are you done flirting? Ready to play?" Theo teased even though she had just finished racking the balls.

"Sorry to keep you waiting, Your Majesty," I said with a mock bow before bending over the table to play.

Soon, the room filled with teasing, the sound of the wooden sticks hitting the balls, and the balls hitting against each other. It was the surround sound I loved, but made even better since it was all my friends in the room for once.

"Remember that first night that we met Kass," Grant said.

"Quite a first impression," Reed said with a nod.

"So, when I win, what are you going to cook me?" I asked Theo as I hit yet another ball into the pocket.

"I think a vegan meal," she teased. "Lot of vegetables."

"Rude," I said and stuck my tongue out at her.

She laughed and we ended up playing two out of three, which I smoked her in both my wins.

With a resigned sigh, she said, "I'll make you some delicious food. Maybe tacos."

I skipped out of the room and back to the bar top where Silver had two drinks waiting for us.

"Judging by your smile and Theo's scowl, I'm going to guess you won?" he asked as he started making another drink for someone.

"Of course I won," I said and flipped my hair over my shoulder, purposefully smacking Theo with it.

She sputtered as the hair hit her face and pinched my arm. "Brat."

Laughing, we both clinked our glasses against the other and took a big drink.

I knew this perfect, calm, happy time would have bumps in the future, but I pushed those thoughts out of my mind to enjoy the happy time now.

We would face whatever came, when it came.

"Since this is a closed event in the bar," Theo started and Silver immediately scowled. "Could we order food to eat here?"

He opened his mouth to immediately reject her, took a breath, and said, "You know what, sure. Tonight is to celebrate Kass and her mates and she's been through enough that she deserves food as well. Plus, I'd rather you two not get super drunk while not eating. Tonka!"

Tonka walked over, a drink in his hand, the first time I had ever seen the bouncer drink. "Yeah, boss?"

"Can you go get forty tacos from the restaurant and bring them back?" Silver asked and pulled a wad of cash out of his pocket. "Make sure you get salsa, too."

Tonka chugged his drink, set the empty glass down, and nodded as he took the glass. "Sure thing."

"If you don't want tacos, get yourself something else," Silver ordered him.

Tonka smiled. "Tacos are good."

"I knew we were friends for a reason," I teased him.

He winked at me and headed to go get us tacos.

"Did ... did Tonka just wink at Kass? Are ... are they actually friends now?" Theo sat hard on the barstool. "I think I might faint."

I rolled my eyes at her. "How dare you. I'm very likeable. It was only a matter of time before he stopped pretending to hate me."

Silver shook his head as he cleaned a glass. "He never hated you. He just hated that you made his job harder."

"I didn't do it on purpose," I muttered.

"So, what are your future plans, old man?" Theo asked Silver.

He set the glass down and said, "The girls and I were actually talking about going on a trip."

"A trip?" I asked, eyes wide.

He nodded. "We've not gone on a family trip in far too long. I think we're going to go visit my homeland, so I can introduce them to my clan and visit my people. Plus, I want to take them to meet their people, to meet other trolls in hopes they might find their mates. As much as they claim they're happy, I know they'd be even happier with mates of their own."

What he said made sense. I hadn't thought about the twins not having as many potential mates here since the trolls tended to stay secluded from the rest of the world. "What about the bar?" I asked. If he closed it, I wasn't sure what I would do with myself. I loved this place and all the people who frequented here. It was a second home, which made me sound like a lush, but it was less about the drinking and more about the comradery.

He smiled at me. "I've heard a rumor that you've learned to be quite a good manager and I know you owe me and would love to order Tonka around a bit. So, I'd hoped you would handle things while I was gone. I found a bartender who can serve drinks while you manage the rest of it."

Wow, he really had thought all this through.

"You aren't retiring on us, are you?" Theo asked.

"Not yet, but soon. I am, as you two like to so often remind me, an old man. It's about time for me to retire and relax."

"He already talked to me about it and I have someone I was interviewing for assistant manager already," Gina said, coming up behind us. "I think they could handle the pizza place while you handle things here, Kass."

"I would be honored to manage the bar while you and the twins go on your trip," I said. "How long do you think you'll be gone?"

"I'm planning for two weeks, but it depends on if the twins find any potential mates," he said.

Theo and I lapsed into silence, drinking and watching the people around us, lost in our thoughts about all of these changes coming to our lives. Change was scary, but sometimes it was also good. Thinking back to Theo and I being in this bar four years ago, running our pool scams on the tourists and spending time together, they were good memories. However, looking at where we were now, it was even better. As scary as change could be, I was looking forward to seeing where we ended up four years from now.

"I hope they'll find mates," Theo whispered. "They both deserve to find love after everything they've been through."

I nodded. "Exactly. Those two have been through so much. It's definitely their turn to find a mate, or mates. Whatever floats their boats."

"Says the shark who liked to sink boats," Theo teased.

"That was one time and they were killing sharks for no reason," I countered.

"I didn't say they didn't deserve it," she said and laughed.

The door to the bar opened. My mouth parted in excitement, thinking it was Tonka with our tacos, but instead, Cap'n Two-Teeth and his Chums entered, all with their top halfs shifted into their shark forms, but their bottom halfs with human legs.

"Cap'n!" I yelled, even more excited than I had been about the tacos.

"Kass!" he and his crew yelled.

I rushed forward to hug the pirate shark shifters.

Cap'n Two-Teeth, his upper half was that of a great white shark with a hook in his dorsal fin that was no longer rusted, which made me happy.

"Your hook's not rusted anymore. Does that mean you're not sick now?" I asked, though, I hadn't asked when it was rusted if it had been because he was sick, since I hadn't wanted to pry.

"Turns out I had a curse on me, but I got it lifted," he said with a shrug. "Well, that one lifted." He smiled, showing his two teeth in his gums.

"It's good to see you," I said. "I'm sorry I haven't been down to visit."

He scoffed. "You're mated now and working. We understand." At my wide eyes he said, "We ask about you and keep tabs to make sure you're doing alright."

I hugged him again. "Thanks."

"Congratulations on being mated, by the way. We were all getting worried about you, but it makes this old heart happy to know you've got mates." He scowled as he looked at said mates, who were walking out of the pool room and towards us. "Though, I wish they were aquatic."

If it weren't for him, I wouldn't have made it this far in life. Turning, I said, "Silver, a round for the Cap'n and his crew on me, please."

The chums all cheered and headed to the bar to get their drinks.

"You doing alright? No more crazy battles?" Cap'n asked as we joined the crew at the bar.

I laughed. "Hopefully not, but I'm always on alert, just in case. Never know how many enemies are still lurking out there."

"Well, if you ever need anything, you just call on us," Cap'n said.

"I appreciate that. And that offer goes for you as well. If you and your crew ever need anything, you let me know. We sharks need to stick together," I said.

"How about an arm-wrestling match?" Shamus challenged with a wide smile. The older great white was always challenging me to matches of some sort. He was the first mate and enjoyed displays of strength.

"Oh, you're on, old man!" I replied and moved to a nearby high table, setting my elbow on top of it, and wiggled my fingers.

Shamus chugged his beer, walked over, and we clasped hands, elbows on the table. "You ready to lose, tiger?"

"In your dreams, basic white." I smiled, showing my teeth as I used the insult. He was a great white shark, but I liked to call him basic because it irked him.

"I've got twenty on Kass," Grant said as he joined us and slapped a bill on the bar top.

"I'll take that bet!" Trent, a hammerhead shark, said and slapped his bill on top of Grant's.

All of the Chums started placing bets and it wasn't long before the rest of my friends joined in as well.

"Ready?" I asked Shamus.

"I'm not getting any younger," he teased.

Reed set his hand atop our joined ones and said, "Ready? Go!" As soon as he released our hands, Shamus and I clenched, trying to push the other down.

"You've gotten weaker, tiger," Shamus grunted.

"Have I? You're the one who seems to be struggling." I yawned and tapped my free hand against my mouth.

Shamus growled and gripped the table with his other hand, now trying harder.

So, I gripped the table and started pulling the back of his hand down towards the tabletop.

Everyone cheered for who they bet on, some calling

insults to "shark up" while others called words of encouragement.

With one more hard jerk, I slammed the back of his hand against the table, released it, and threw my arms up in victory.

"Kass, thirty and Shamus, zero!" I shouted. "How's it feel to get defeated thirty times in a row?"

"I swear she cheats," Shamus said as he rubbed his arm.

"How about darts?" I challenged.

His eyes sparkled. "Bring it!"

Tonka walked in carrying several bags and the scent of tacos immediately hit me.

"After tacos," I said and Shamus nodded his agreement, rubbing his hands together at the scent.

Everyone got into a line to get some tacos.

Jong-min kissed my cheek as he stood beside me, smiling down at me. My formerly grumpy cat shifter male was much less grumpy ever since we'd officially become mates.

Grant stepped up behind me and kissed the side of my neck, right over his mark, making me shiver in delight.

Reed looped his arm around my waist and squeezed me against his side.

Not to be left out, Jong-hyun walked over, stooped in front of me, and placed a chaste kiss on my lips, giving me a wink before he turned around.

"Hey! No cutting," I accused him.

"I'm protecting your front," he replied.

Rolling my eyes, I stepped out of my mates' holds and stepped in front of him. "No, you're trying to get tacos before me. I thought we decided as a pack that I always get to eat first?"

"No, you tried to enact that and we all declined," Jong-min countered.

"You said you'd rather I ate first, so you didn't have to deal with me being hangry," I reminded him.

"I said that for that day because you were being exceptionally hangry," he countered back.

After filling up our plates, everyone sat together, eating, teasing each other, and enjoying the delicious food.

This was everything I had ever wanted.

This was my true, happily ever after.

EPILOGUE

"Who stole the tray of cookies?" Theo shouted. "Cassandra, was it you?"

"It wasn't me, Mom!" she shouted back from the couch beside me, quickly shoving the last cookie into her mouth and chewing it as fast as she could to hide the evidence. Cassandra was four years old, a mage, had bright red, curly hair, and had been adopted by Theo and her mates three years ago. I absolutely spoiled the crap out of the adorable girl. I spoiled all of my nieces and nephews.

She wasn't lying about not stealing the cookies. I had stolen the cookie tray and shared my spoils with all five of my nieces and nephews.

It was crazy how four years could bring so much change. Four years after my mating party, I now had three nieces and two nephews.

"Kass!" Zyra gasped. "You know you can't give them cookies before dinner!"

Illa and Tanjin, my niece and nephew respectively, both

three years old, with the cutest little troll tusks, pouted behind their mother as she scolded me.

"I don't know what you mean," I said and took a sip from my drink.

Zara pushed Aketa and Zulkaz, my twin niece and nephew, into the room, crumbs all over their adorable two-year-old faces. "Kass," she growled. Zara saw Zyra and the kids and sighed, shaking her head.

Standing, I wiped my hands on my jeans and smiled wide. "Who is ready for dinner?"

"We are!" all my nieces and nephews yelled and we all ran to the dining room in a planned out, synchronized move. Now, Zara and Zyra were left grumbling in the other room and Theo just sighed and shook her head.

That sighing and head shaking happened a lot when I was around my family.

The kids sat at their smaller table and I sat with them. I preferred eating at the kids' table.

Silver walked in and patted all of the kids on the heads as he passed and even patted mine, making me smile up at him.

Grant, Reed, Jong-min, Jong-hyun, Zyra, Zara, Zara's mate, Kuroji, Zyra's mate, Venjo, Theo, Damien, Tristan, Antoine, and Silver sat at the adult table.

Theo had tried to purchase a large table for holiday dinners such as this, ensuring there was enough seating for all of the adults. However, there were so many of us that Damien had ended up building one for us instead. It had taken them a full year to find a house that fit their needs and even then, they'd made adjustments to their first floor so the dining room was large enough for the huge table, and for the living room to be large enough to fit enough couches for us all to sit when we met. Normally, we also had Jong-kyu and his mate, Mi-Yong, with us, but they had returned to their homeland to visit his family.

We took turns hosting and next year was my turn. I had an easier time finding a location, since Silver had sold the bar to me and I could close it down to have our family events there.

"How's the bar doing?" Silver asked as if he could tell I was thinking about it.

"Doing really well," I said.

"She conned an entire basketball team and made over a thousand dollars in a single night," Grant said, ratting me out.

"Tattletale!" I hissed at him.

"Snitches get stitches," Cassandra muttered before she shoveled some cooked chicken into her mouth.

"Cassandra!" Antoine snapped.

I put another bread roll onto her plate, earning a big smile from her and a scowl from Theo and her mates.

Kuroji and Venjo, whispered conspiratorially together, which did not bode well for me. The two troll males liked tormenting me and playing pranks on me. My own mates joined in often, too, especially Reed.

"Auntie," Tanjin whispered.

I looked over at him.

He leaned across the table, trying to get closer and whispered, "Don't drink what Da brings you."

My eyes widened. Tanjin must have overheard what his dad and uncle were planning. What a great nephew!

I winked and put a bread roll on his plate. "Thanks, buddy."

He tore into his bread while smiling, his little tusks glistening with melted butter now.

"Let's have a toast," Silver said and stood.

"We got it, Father," Venjo said as he and Kuroji stood. Kuroji passed out glasses while Venjo went to get the sparkling wine bottles from the kitchen.

Kuroji set a glass in front of me and I held it up, inspecting it, but there was nothing inside ... yet.

Venjo poured glasses for everyone, including himself, leaving me for last. As he poured it, I heard the soft clink of him dropping something into the glass first right before he poured the wine.

Clever bastard!

I stood, carrying my glass with me as I made my way over to the adult table. I leaned my elbows on Reed's shoulders, swirling my glass with a smile as I waited for Silver to make his toast. I set my glass down right next to Reed's, set my hands on his shoulders, and leaned over to kiss his cheek.

He glanced at me, but when I just smiled at him, he returned the smile and turned as Silver stood.

Silver raised his glass. "To family. No matter what life may throw at us, we'll be together and will help each other through it all."

I quickly grabbed Reed's glass and raised it, smiling wide. "To family!" I shouted.

We all clinked our glasses together and took a drink of the sparkling wine.

Reed immediately sputtered as the tablet caused him to foam at the mouth.

I laughed so hard I grabbed my stomach and doubled over.

"How did you know?" Venjo demanded.

I tapped my ear. "I heard the soft clink of the pill. You almost got me, though."

Reed chugged his water to clear out the pill's effects. "You brat," he growled at me.

"Serves you right for all the times you've teamed up with them against me."

As we made our way to the living room for games and dessert, I slipped an extra cookie onto Tanjin's plate.

He gasped, eyes wide, and I winked at him. "My informants are always paid well."

"What happened to, 'snitches get stitches?'" Jong-hyun teased.

I screeched in surprise, not having heard him sneak up on me. Spinning around, I sweetly said, "That's only when it's against me."

He slid his arms around my waist and nuzzled my cheek before whispering in my ear, "You're such a naughty auntie."

"Ew! No kissing!" Aketa and Zulkaz yelled simultaneously. The twins often spoke and acted at the same time. Their twin bond was similar to Jong-min and Jong-hyun, but stronger since they were younger.

"You're no fun!" I teased them, spun and held out my arms. "Can I get hugs from you then?"

They yelped and ran away from me.

"Come back! Auntie wants hugs!" I yelled as I chased them around the living room.

"You're going to tickle us!" they yelled over their shoulders.

"I would never!" I gasped.

Jong-min caught me around the waist, pulling me onto his lap on the couch. "Stop tormenting the children. It's late and they need to let their food digest first."

"Spoilsport," I sighed.

"I challenge Kass to charades!" Antoine said as we debated what games to play.

"Can't handle how badly I defeated you last time?" I asked.

"You lost," he said.

"That's not how I remember it," I countered.

"That's because you were hammered," Theo countered back.

I gasped and put a hand to my chest. "Are you taking your mate's side instead of mine? What kind of best friend are you?"

"Telling the truth isn't taking sides," she said and rolled her eyes.

"I think we should play teams," Silver said. "I'm pretty confident Theo, Antoine, and I can defeat Kass, Zyra, and Kuroji."

Zyra scoffed. "You can't defeat me at anything, old man."

He smiled, knowing he had her. "Prove it then."

We spent the next two hours playing charades, laughing, and eating dessert. As the kids grew tired, we said our good-byes to head home.

"Still on for tacos Wednesday?" Theo asked.

"You know it!" I hugged her and each of her mates before skipping down to my waiting mates.

"I'm impressed. You behaved this time," Grant teased as we all buckled into the car.

"She switched her drink with mine," Reed reminded him.

"Yeah, but you deserved it," Jong-hyun teased.

"Ready to head home?" Jong-min asked as he started the car.

I nodded. "Yes. Home sounds great."

"Especially since she knows Jong-hyun stole leftovers and a tray of cookies," Grant said.

I squealed and leaned over to kiss Jong-hyun's cheek. "You're the best!"

"Don't forget it," he said with a wink and a smile.

"To second dinner and dessert at home!" I shouted and pointed out the front window.

My mates rolled their eyes, but all of them smiled as they did just that.

If you enjoyed this duet, check out my complete paranormal reverse harem romance, *Her Royal Harem*:

books2read.com/re

Join my newsletter for release information & giveaways:

catbanks.co/NL

CONNECT WITH CATHERINE BANKS

I really appreciate you reading my book! Here are some ways to connect with me:
www.catherinebanks.com

Join my newsletter for deals and snippets:
http://catbanks.co/newsletter

ABOUT THE AUTHOR

Catherine Banks is a USA Today bestselling fantasy author who writes in several fantasy subgenres and has multiple pseudonyms. She began writing fiction at only four years old and finished her first full-length novel at the age of fifteen. She is married to her soulmate and best friend, Avery, who she has two amazing children with. After her full-time job, she reads books, plays video games, and watches anime shows and movies with her family to relax. Although she has lived in Northern California her entire life, she dreams of traveling around the world. Catherine is also C.E.O. of Turbo Kitten Industries™, a company with many hats including being a book publisher and Etsy store full of nerdy fun.

facebook.com/catherinebanksauthor

amazon.com/author/catherinebanks

bookbub.com/authors/catherine-banks